ANCELL'S QUEST

Angell's Quest

Tony Main

Copyright © 2015 Tony Main

The moral right of the author has been asserted.

Apart from any fair dealing for the purposes of research or private study, or criticism or review, as permitted under the Copyright, Designs and Patents Act 1988, this publication may only be reproduced, stored or transmitted, in any form or by any means, with the prior permission in writing of the publishers, or in the case of reprographic reproduction in accordance with the terms of licences issued by the Copyright Licensing Agency. Enquiries concerning reproduction outside those terms should be sent to the publishers.

Matador
9 Priory Business Park
Kibworth Beauchamp
Leicestershire LE8 0RX, UK
Tel: (+44) 116 279 2299
Fax: (+44) 116 279 2277
Email: books@troubador.co.uk
Web: www.troubador.co.uk/matador

ISBN 978 1784622 039

British Library Cataloguing in Publication Data.
A catalogue record for this book is available from the British Library.

Printed and bound in the UK by TJ International, Padstow, Cornwall
Typeset in Book Antiqua by Troubador Publishing Ltd

Matador is an imprint of Troubador Publishing Ltd

For Nancy, Charlie, Ellie and Elsie,
and with grateful thanks to SJW and SJS

'…the dreamers of the day are dangerous men, for they may act out their dreams with open eyes, to make it possible.'

TE Lawrence

CHAPTER 1

Ancell was fighting for his life. His assailant struck yet again and he stumbled, curling tightly and whimpering with pain. Suddenly he was tumbling through space. He seemed to fall for a long time until he awoke with a jolt and lay trembling until he recognised the familiar surroundings of his nest.

The dreams were not always the same. Sometimes he clung to a storm-tossed ship swept by icy seas. Sometimes he was crawling across a never-ending desert beneath a blazing sun. But there was always the tearful voice of someone in distress. A vaguely familiar voice he could not place – someone far away south across the oceans begging for his help. Someone who was very afraid.

'Why me?' he muttered, shuffling round in circles. 'I'm just an ordinary hedgehog. I'm no adventurer. I've never even been to sea. What help can I be?'

But he knew he had no choice. If he were ever to sleep with an easy heart he had to seek whoever called him so urgently. The beech wood stirred, whispering there was no time to lose. He could delay no longer. He took a last look at his nest, wondering if he would ever see his home again, and stepped from the protection of the trees.

Day and night he travelled south, keeping to the foot of hedgerows and often stopping to sniff and listen for danger. Once he followed a country lane and had to scuttle aside when a stagecoach pulled by four galloping horses hurtled by, the ruddy-faced coachman cracking his whip and yelling at him to get out of the way. But at last, wearily breasting a hill on the morning of the sixth day, he finally gazed down upon the sea sparkling in the sunshine - the ripples of blue stretching far, far away, mysterious and waiting.

The port was crowded with masts towering high above the wharves where gangs of sweating men hurried to load and unload cargoes. Often knocked aside, he boarded ship after ship begging a passage south, only to be rebuffed with a scornful laugh and told to clear off. Glumly watching the thrashing paddle wheels of a tug towing a great four-masted vessel seaward, he noticed a last ship lying alongside a deserted quay. No more than ninety feet long and with a beam of twenty feet she looked small and tubby. She had two masts, a bluff bow with a long bowsprit, and on her square stern he read the paint flaked name, "Misty Dawn". The ebbing tide had left her lying at an ungainly angle on the mud, and though sturdily built she appeared forlorn and abandoned - a ship that had sailed many seas, but now her work was done would soon be towed to the breaker's yard.

A sea otter climbed from below. His weather-beaten face and pale blue eyes told of a lifetime of long voyages to distant lands.

'Ahoy there! Can I help you?' he called, removing his peak cap to reveal a head of hair as grey as his whiskers. Ancell immediately felt he was someone he could trust.

'I'm seeking a passage south.'

The sea otter studied him. 'And why would that be?'

Ancell felt the all-knowing eyes pierce his innermost thoughts. He would have to speak the truth. Nervously he told of the unknown voice begging for his help from some sun-parched land far to the south. The sea otter did not laugh.

'And you are determined on your quest?' he asked. 'The Southern Continent is a long voyage. You will find it hard.'

'Even so,' replied Ancell firmly, 'I have to find whoever is calling me.'

The sea otter leaned on the ship's rail and gazed far out to sea. 'Then it is the task of Misty to see you follow your dream,' he murmured. He faced Ancell. 'I am Captain Morgan Albern, Master of "Misty Dawn". You'd better come below.'

Ancell looked about the captain's warm, homely cabin. A brassbound barometer and clock hung on one wall, below which, volumes of tide tables and navigation manuals were crammed on shelves behind wooden fiddles to hold them in place in rough weather. A separate shelf was lined with the music of the great composers.

'The passage to the Southern Ocean and Australia is westward round Cape Horn,' said the captain, unrolling the charts. It seemed to Ancell that most of the world was sea.

'Don't you think,' he said, 'I mean I was just wondering if your ship is a bit small…' He was going to add, 'and old,' but stopped short at the sea otter's glare. Even so Capt. Albern's reply was patient.

'Misty and I have circumnavigated the world together for many years. There is not an ocean on the globe she does not understand.' He patted the chart table. 'Never have I known a ship that listens to the wind so well.'

'Captain, Sir, please give me a berth,' pleaded Ancell.

The sea otter regarded him gravely and nodded.

'Mostly I'm called Skipper,' he said.

Ancell wandered on deck and casually stood behind the wheel. With a quick glance ashore to check no one was looking, he took hold of the spokes and swayed to an imaginary swell as he steered Misty across the oceans. A discreet cough interrupted his daydream and he turned to face the scruffiest creature he had ever seen. It had a scrawny weasel-like face with deep-set eyes and its straggly fur stuck out in all directions. With a withered arm and a long sniff, the crossbreed extended a mug of steaming tea.

'Skipper said you might like this,' he said, staring at Ancell holding the helm.

'Thank you! Thank you indeed!' said Ancell, stepping sharply from behind the wheel.

'And you are?' he asked.

'The Cook,' sighed the animal. 'I am the cook, and that is what I am called.' He glanced at the wheel again.

Ancell blushed. 'I was just sort of getting the feel of it.'

'She steers better when she's afloat,' sniffed The Cook, and with a wipe of his nose limped back to his galley on spindly legs, one of which was substantially shorter than the other.

Ancell spent the evening settling into his cabin, which he thought a little small, furnished only with a bunk, a drop-leafed table screwed to the floor, and a locker in which hung yellow oilskins and a lifejacket. Over a meal of a tasty stew, Capt. Albern asked him nothing more about his quest; he seemed to understand without needing to enquire. The Cook, the sea otter informed him, preferred to eat in the privacy of his galley, and, apart from being a very good cook – who made an excellent treacle tart – kept watch on Misty in port. Misty was his home.

Ancell twice singed himself lighting the oil lamp above his bunk, which was as cosy as his nest after he had slotted into place the board to stop him falling out in heavy seas. He felt a momentary pang of homesickness for the familiar woods and hedgerows he had left behind, and then with a thrill sensed Misty lift from the mud on the rising tide. He watched the lamplight flit about the cabin as she tugged gently on her mooring lines and wondered about Capt. Albern who could read his dreams. The voice was calling him again. He thought it sounded a little less plaintive, as if knowing he was on his way, but still urging him to hurry.

'I'm coming,' he whispered. 'I'll find you, I promise.'

CHAPTER 2

Misty's decks were already warm with the morning sun when Ancell awoke. A kettle steamed in the galley, which was as spotlessly clean and ordered as The Cook was dishevelled.

'I suppose you want something to eat?' said The Cook with a sigh.

'If you wouldn't mind,' said Ancell, and was rewarded with a bowl of porridge. Over a mug of tea, The Cook told him that Capt. Albern was ashore arranging for the ship's officers to join, shortly to be followed by the crew. Ancell wondered what they would think of a landlubber searching for an unknown voice somewhere on the other side of the world.

'What are they like?' he asked anxiously.

'The best! The skipper's the best, so he chooses who he wants. No one turns down a voyage on Misty - and they won't mind a passenger.'

Ancell considered himself more important than a mere passenger, but said nothing.

'Ahoy there!' called Capt. Albern, and Ancell turned to see the hump back of the sea otter lolloping up the gangplank. While The Cook brewed more tea, the captain informed them that all the crew he wished to recruit would sail, though he had yet to find Chad, the ship's bosun. Miss Strait, at whose boarding house he lodged, had not seen him for two days.

The Cook sighed. 'Probably under a table in some bar.'

'Maybe,' agreed the captain, 'but for this voyage it's essential I have him on board. I'll call again this evening.'

Ancell was curious to meet so crucial a member of the ship's company.

'May I come with you?' he asked.

'Good idea!' said The Cook. 'You can help carry him back.'

It was already dark when Ancell followed Capt. Albern ashore and the streets were quiet apart from the clatter of hooves on cobblestones as a youth led a horse to a stable. The sea otter set a steady pace, stopping only once to drop a coin into the palm of a young girl selling matches. Her pale face looked up gratefully as she pulled the thin shawl about her shoulders more tightly.

Miss Strait's establishment was distinguished by brightly planted window boxes and a notice displaying the rates for her rooms, together with a list of house rules which concluded with the warning that unruly behaviour would not be tolerated.

Capt. Albern pulled on the bell chain and a severe looking woman, wearing a black dress and white lace bonnet, ushered them into the kitchen.

'Any sign of him, Ma'am?' asked the captain.

Miss Strait shook her head. A flicker of misgiving crossed her face.

'I suppose it's another voyage,' she said.

Capt. Albern took her by the shoulders. 'Yes Ma'am, an important one.'

Miss Strait stirred a bubbling stew. 'Perhaps it's as well,' she said softly. 'He gets bored. Will you be gone long?'

'It will be a while.'

'You will bring him back?'

'I'll do that,' promised the captain.

Miss Strait dabbed her eyes with the corner of her apron. 'It's the onions,' she explained.

Following Miss Strait's directions to the "Flag and Anchor", where Chad was most likely to be found, Capt. Albern and Ancell crossed a bridge over a river into a maze of narrow alleyways. A gang of barefoot boys idly watched them. One threw a stone and they laughed when Ancell stumbled in his hurry to get away.

The windows of the "Flag and Anchor" were curtained, but through a broken pane, Ancell could hear raucous voices and the chink of glasses. A man began to sing and others joined in a drunken chorus.

'Let's hope you're in there,' murmured the captain as they paused outside.

At that moment the swing doors burst open and a body of flailing arms and legs shot through the air.

'Out you go!' laughed two burly men, inspecting their knuckles as the body slid to a halt. For a moment the riotous clamour of the drinkers spilled into the night, then the doors swung shut and the street was silent again. The body was a sinewy Common rat, brown backed and greying towards its under-parts, with a tail nearly as long as itself. The tail twitched and it pulled itself up with the aid of a lamppost. It brushed itself down, took a deep breath, and staggered purposefully for the door.

'Hello, Chad,' said Capt. Albern.

The rat span round, 'Skipper!' he cried, grabbing the sea otter with delight and for support. 'Come and have a drink.'

'I think not. It's time to go.'

'Whatever you say, Skipper. Just give me a couple of minutes to sort out a little matter.'

Capt. Albern sighed as the rat took one step back, two to one side, steadied himself, and lurched for the entrance. Ancell moved to hold him back but Capt. Albern stayed his arm. The doors swung shut. There was a moment's silence and then an uproar of yells and curses followed by the crash of upturned tables. The doors flew open again and once more the rat landed in the street. Ancell noticed that on this occasion the two men were not laughing. One was nursing a bloody nose and the other a rapidly swelling eye.

'Satisfied?' enquired Capt. Albern, helping Chad to his feet.

'Someone called me plague-ridden vermin. Nobody gets away with that,' Chad informed him.

'Yersinia pestis.'

'That wasn't his name.'

'Yersinia pestis is the bacterium of the Black Death, carried by fleas and rats,' explained Capt. Albern. 'However it was black rats that spread the disease.'

'That is exactly what I intended to say when I hit him,' replied Chad.

Ancell followed a few paces behind the two seafarers, who appeared to have forgotten of his existence. Chad stopped at the river.

'Skipper, there's a hedgehog following us,' he whispered in the captain's ear, glancing at Ancell from the corner of his eye. Capt. Albern apologised profusely for forgetting to introduce them.

'Ancell is sailing with us,' he told Chad.

'Did you say sailing! And did you say us!'

'Misty is sailing for the Southern Ocean. Why else do you think I'm here?'

'A voyage at last!' shouted Chad, and with a

leap was running along the parapet of the bridge, arms outstretched to keep his far-from-certain balance.

'He won't fall off,' Capt. Albern assured Ancell.

Ancell looked down at the dark water swirling beneath the arches and wished the rat did just that. So much for an important member of the crew, he thought. A has-been, who drinks too much, picks fights in bars, and worst of all, who had not even acknowledged his presence. This, Chad corrected when they caught up with him, though not as Ancell would have wished.

'You're a greenhorn, aren't you?' he announced.

'I'm not a sailor, if that's what you mean,' replied Ancell stiffly.

'No need to get prickly about it,' mocked Chad with a giggle.

'But he has a purpose. We need to take him south,' interceded Capt. Albern.

'You don't look very purposeful,' Chad told Ancell. 'It's just as well you found Misty. We'll look after you.'

Ancell was not reassured.

Chad paused outside Miss Strait's door.

'Just get my gear,' he said. 'Keep quiet; don't want to wake her.'

Chad had nearly reached the top of the stairs when Miss Strait called his name. The rat froze.

'Tell her I'm not here,' he whispered.

'Chad's here,' announced Capt. Albern. 'My apologies Ma'am for keeping you up so late.'

Miss Strait appeared from her kitchen. With a despairing glance at his skipper, Chad tiptoed down to face her. Hands on hips, Miss Strait first listed the rat's many character flaws. This was followed by a summary of his bad habits, which featured laying in bed half the morning, frequenting bars of ill repute, compromising the good name of her establishment and failing to put his dirty laundry in the basket provided for that very purpose.

'Well spoken, Ma'am,' intoned Capt. Albern in a graveside manner.

Chad then learned that undeserving though he was, she had washed and ironed his clothes and a freshly baked fruitcake was packed in his sea-bag. Chad kissed her hand and Ancell noticed her blush.

It was midnight before they climbed back on board. Ancell slept fitfully, and in his dreams saw a figure standing over him aiming a pistol. He watched the finger tighten on the trigger and flinched. There was a flash and a bang and he started awake to see sunlight flitting through the porthole of his cabin and hear the sound of hammering on deck.

CHAPTER 3

The source of the noise was a rotund beaver who talked to himself as he worked. His outer coat was of shiny reddish brown hair, through which Ancell glimpsed a beautiful silver tinged under-fur. He had broad protruding front teeth and a balding head, on top of which miraculously perched a bowler hat several sizes too small. A group of figures stood about the galley, sipping mugs of tea and chatting in the easy fashion of old shipmates. Ancell was wondering if he dare ask The Cook for something to eat, when a red squirrel, tall and well groomed with a fine bushy tail, caught sight of him. The squirrel ducked into the galley and presented him with a thick slice of bread and jam.

'Something to keep you going – I gather you missed breakfast,' he said. 'Welcome aboard! My name is Truegard, Misty's first mate. I understand you wish to travel south.'

There was such an air of calm authority about the squirrel that Ancell felt a renewed strength of purpose just by standing in his presence. Without hesitation he told of his quest.

Truegard listened intently. 'How did you come to find Misty?'

'By chance I thought. But Capt. Albern seemed to be waiting for me.'

The first mate looked seaward. 'Perhaps he was. I had a feeling this was more than just another voyage,' he murmured. 'I'll introduce you to the crew.'

Ancell first met Waff, the sailmaker, an ageing and rather mangey polecat with tobacco stained fur. Waff acknowledged him with a grunt while stitching a sail and puffing on a pipe clenched hard between his teeth. The beaver immediately joined them.

'And this is Chips, the ship's carpenter,' said Truegard.

'You want to keep upwind of that pipe,' Chips advised Ancell. 'In fact you want to keep upwind of Waff when he's in a tizz. She's a fine ship you're sailing on, and if I may say, maintained by the finest of carpenters.' The taciturn sailmaker sighed.

'Mind you, I can't vouch for the sails,' continued Chips, 'even though anyone could stitch a bit of canvas. Have you heard how I once repaired a rudder stock in the middle of an Atlantic gale?'

Waff's shoulders slumped. 'Not again! Not that story again!' he groaned to Truegard. 'Take him away and give him something useful to do so I can get some work done.'

'If you worked like a beaver, you'd have done it by now,' retorted Chips.

Truegard laughed and walked on.

'Seems like you've got trouble with those two,' remarked Ancell. Truegard's large brown eyes regarded him with amazement.

'Chips and Waff are the oldest of friends. Chips is alone and always spends his shore leave with Waff's family. Chips puts up with Waff's pipe, and Waff with Chips's chatter – apart from which I think we can rely upon the skipper to select a suitable crew.'

Ancell blushed at the gentle rebuke.

'And here's Skeet, our second mate,' said Truegard, as a whirl of brown fur with a white belly and black tipped tail bounded towards them. The stoat rushed up to the first mate, slapping Waff on the back and tipping Chips's bowler over his eyes in passing.

'Have you decided the watches?' he panted. Truegard introduced Ancell.

'Pleased to have you with us – the more the merrier,' said Skeet. 'Now, Mr Truegard, which of the crew are you putting on my watch? And do you want me to take the first watch or the second? And how soon can we sail? And when...'

'Steady there! All in good time,' said Truegard. 'Mr Skeet is young and in a hurry,' he told Ancell. 'When he learns to slow down he'll make a good first mate.'

'You're always saying that,' said Skeet.

'And you're still always in a hurry,' said Truegard, and they both laughed.

Ancell watched the two stroll away, the stoat still bombarding the red squirrel with questions.

The Cook beckoned him to the galley. Ancell hoped he was to be offered a late breakfast.

'As you're not doing anything you can help unpack these crates,' said The Cook.

Ancell settled to the task.

'Where's Chad?' he asked, expecting to be told the rat was sleeping off a hangover.

'He's been ashore since daybreak ordering equipment for the ship.'

Ancell prised open another crate. He was not sure whether he was pleased at the bosun's powers of recovery or disappointed he was not languishing on his bunk suffering a thoroughly deserved headache.

'What's this?' he asked, wrinkling his nose.

'Sauerkraut. It helps stave off scurvy.'

'And why all these jars of treacle? What's that going to save us from?'

'Nothing! The skipper's partial to it.'

Hails of welcome announced the arrival of two youthful long-tailed field mice, one male, one female, their sea bags slung easily across their shoulders. Everyone seemed pleased to see them and receive a nod of greeting.

'Tamlan and Thomasina,' said The Cook.

'A female member of the crew?' queried Ancell.

'There's no one fitter or a better sailor than Thom. I doubt anyone can match her on the helm, though Tam comes close. They're twins, and where Thom goes, Tam goes.'

'They don't say much.'

'Habit, I suppose. They know what the other is thinking. When they're hanging on a yard in a gale at night they instinctively know what the other is doing. They'd know if they were oceans apart.'

'Are there any other crew?'

'Pickle and Jobey - and they're late.'

It was mid afternoon before the two sailors climbed on board. Both were field mice, though lacking the fine physique of Tam and Thom. Pickle beamed happily and Jobey scowled at the deck whilst Chad berated them for failing to report on time. Pickle's excuse was that he was so looking forward to sailing with the bosun again he had stopped off for a celebratory drink, and Jobey's that he had first had to have something to eat on the assumption The Cook would be too mean to provide a lunch.

The following days saw Misty transformed. Chips, talking to anyone passing within earshot of his workbench, sawed and planed amidst piles of wood shavings. Waff sewed in silence, surrounded by rolls of canvas. Tam and Thom worked together, sheathing the hull with an outer skin of planking to protect against tropical worms. Pickle, smelling of pitch and whistling cheerfully, caulked the decks, and Jobey wire brushed rust and painted while complaining he had been allocated the worst job. Chad was everywhere, at one moment working high on a yard, the next swinging from the bow in a bosun's chair. Skeet scurried ashore on errands, leaping back on board as if Misty was about to cast off, and in the midst of all the activity, Truegard inspected, encouraged, and calmly solved the occasional problem.

Finally the fresh provisions were loaded, and last of all a cask of rum.

'We won't starve,' Ancell observed, as he helped The Cook stow the fruit and vegetables, pickled eggs, salted pork and hard baked bread.

'It's a long way to the other side of the world,' grunted The Cook.

'When will we get to Australia?'

'Four months maybe - never if a Cape Horn gale drives us onto the rocks.'

Ancell suddenly felt sick with fear. It seemed if he didn't die of scurvy he was likely to drown. Slipping ashore he wandered along the quay, his stomach churning. He could not abandon whoever was calling for his help, yet now Misty was ready to sail all he wanted was to go home. Leaning on a bollard, he felt his shoulder gripped firmly and looked into the kindly eyes of the red squirrel.

'Second thoughts?' asked Truegard.

Ancell nodded miserably.

'Everyone gets nervous at the start of a voyage, but you must follow your dream.'

'It's so far. I might never return.'

'I'm sure you will,' replied Truegard, gently leading Ancell back to the ship.

'And you? You're certain you'll come back?' persisted Ancell.

Truegard gazed seaward. 'Who knows?' he murmured.

'Then why sail?'

Truegard smiled. 'That's easy,' he said. 'The skipper asked me.'

The sun was setting before Capt. Albern made his final inspection of the ship and announced they would cast off at five in the morning.

'Bit early! I was hoping for a lie in,' grumbled Jobey, as the sailors lounged on deck while Pickle strummed a battered guitar.

'Who on earth is that!' exclaimed Skeet. Everyone turned to stare at a large tawny owl attempting to drag a heavy trunk up the gangplank. The bird staggered on board, tripped over a coil of rope, and sat down hard.

'May I help you?' enquired Truegard, lifting him to his feet. The owl regained a semblance of dignity and drew himself up to his full height.

One of his wings was broken and lay across his ample stomach, lending him a Napoleonic stance. He balanced a pince-nez on his large yellow bill and peered through the glasses at the red squirrel.

'Dr Eugene Beaufoy at your service and who wishes to sail with you,' he boomed. 'Kindly direct me to your captain.'

Truegard found Capt. Albern poring over a chart in his cabin.

'Excuse me, Skipper, but there's an owl come aboard asking for a berth - says he's a doctor.'

The sea otter momentarily looked perplexed, but considered.

'A medic on board would be of use, Mr Truegard, and his night vision should be good. Show him down.'

Puffing and grunting, the owl slipped on the companionway steps and sprawled into the captain's cabin. The sea otter inspected him thoughtfully.

'I understand you wish to sail with us. Why should that be?'

'Knowledge, Sir! I seek knowledge of this great wide world,' replied the owl, and reeled off the lands he had visited in the pursuit of his studies.

Capt. Albern smiled. 'I am a plain sailor of not much learning. This will be a long voyage; hardships lie ahead.'

The owl touched his bad wing. 'Frostbite! Got caught in a Siberian winter, but I survived. I implore you to give me a berth. I assure you I'll not get in the way.'

'We do have a spare cabin,' admitted the captain. 'Truegard will show you the way.'

On deck, "Doc", as he was immediately christened, became the subject of intense speculation. Chips was delighted to have someone else to talk to, and The Cook, with a sniff, resigned himself to feeding another mouth. Jobey was convinced the doctor was a charlatan fleeing the country.

'Mark my words,' he warned, 'the moment we climb into our bunks we'll all be arrested for aiding and abetting a criminal.'

Heartened by Truegard's words of encouragement, Ancell retired to his cabin impatient for the voyage to begin. He thought the newcomer an unnecessary hindrance, and anyway Eugene was a ridiculous name for an owl.

CHAPTER 4

Misty cast off in the first light of a chill dawn, and it was far from a seamanlike departure. Pickle dropped the line flung from the tug and then the mooring lines snagged. Chad lost his temper with Jobey for not moving fast enough, and Doc doubled the confusion by flapping about the deck offering advice and getting in everyone's way. Only Truegard remained calm.

Eventually Misty was dragged into clear water, Capt. Albern flinching as her new paintwork scraped along the harbour wall. Ancell would have liked to wave a nonchalant goodbye to a cheering crowd wishing him well, but the quay was deserted other than for a couple of seagulls squabbling over a piece of orange peel. He prepared to meet the owl, who had disentangled himself from a coil of rope, and was approaching fast.

'Pleased to meet you! You must be Ancell. Funny name for a hedgehog,' puffed the owl. Ancell winced.

'Enjoy your trip?' he asked.

'I certainly shall!'

'I was referring to your tumble.'

'Oh that! Nothing serious. You're on this cruise as well I understand.'

Ancell did not classify his mission as a cruise. 'As it happens, I have to travel south,' he replied curtly.

'Another traveller! I'm more than pleased to meet you. I've ranged abroad throughout Europe, visited North West Africa and the Persian Gulf, and once flew to Burma. And you?' Ancell had never ventured more than a mile from his nest.

'Around and about,' he said, steadfastly gazing at the horizon.

Misty objected to being towed. She pulled and jerked at the towline, butting her bow into the seas and straining to break free. At last Capt. Albern uttered the command the crew awaited.

'Cast off and make sail, Mr Truegard. Steer west by south,' he ordered.

The towline was let go, and the tug wished them Godspeed with a series of blasts on its whistle. The main and fore-spencer sails were winched aloft, the foresails set, the topsail and topallant unfurled, and with a kick of delight Misty leaned into a fresh southerly breeze. Ancell thrilled to her easy roll as she picked up speed, occasionally clipping the crest of a wave to send a rattle of spray across her foredeck. There was no going back now, nor did he wish to. He felt himself a sailor already.

It was Chad, who missed nothing, who noticed two eyes peep from beneath the canvas covering the gig, the smaller of the two rowing boats Misty carried.

'We've a stowaway - only a youngster,' he informed Truegard.

The first mate frowned. 'The skipper won't be pleased. We'll have to stop off and put him ashore. Ask him to present himself.'

'He'll come of his own accord once he's cold and hungry enough.'

'He's probably that now; no point in prolonging his misery,' replied Truegard, and went to find the captain.

By the time the sea otter arrived on deck the crew had gathered to watch. Chad yanked off the tarpaulin and leaned into the boat, only to jump back nursing his nose.

'The little imp bit me!' he announced. Everyone laughed.

'Met your match? Need any help?' called Skeet.

'You should have asked him nicely,' said Truegard with a smile.

Chad grabbed again and caught the tip of a tail, on the end of which, squirming and kicking, dangled a young and very small harvest mouse.

'Name?' enquired Capt. Albern.

'Merrie Prentice, Sir, and I want to be a sailor.'

'The Cook will give you something to eat and keep an eye on you until we put you ashore. When we do, you're to go straight home to your parents.'

'Haven't got any, Sir. I want to be a sailor.'

'You'll be safer ashore.'

Tears welled in the harvest mouse's eyes and dribbled down his white front.

'The skipper's right,' Chad told him as he led the way to the galley. 'You can be a sailor when you're a bit older. And don't cry.'

'I'm not crying. The wind's making my eyes water,' sniffed Merrie.

The Cook ladled out a bowl of steaming soup, which Merrie gulped while telling how he had been lucky to escape with his life when the reapers had destroyed the family nest, and that he had been wandering ever since.

'I'd make a good sailor,' he said. 'I could climb a mast as well as anyone.'

'I'm sure you will one day when you're bigger,' agreed The Cook.

'Watch me now!' said Merrie, and ducking under The Cook's restraining arm, leaped onto the ratlines. He climbed quickly to the fore yard and looked down. Beneath him the deck suddenly looked very small, and when Misty rolled he looked down on water. If he looked up, the mast swung across a spinning sky. He closed his eyes, frozen with fear. Tam and Thom worked patiently for half an hour to secure a line round him and lower him to the deck.

'When you climb, you should take it nice and easy,' said Thom.

'Slow and steady,' said Tam.

'I should throw you overboard,' said The Cook, relieved that Capt. Albern had not witnessed the episode.

'I was resting before going up to the top,' replied Merrie. The Cook crouched and looked the harvest mouse hard in the face.

'You can bluff when you're ashore if you want, but not at sea. We need to trust one another for the safety of us all, so never lie.'

'Please let me stay,' implored Merrie. 'I could learn to climb the mast and then I'd be useful.'

'Have you nowhere to go when we put you ashore – no relations, no friends?'

Merrie shook his head. The Cook stared into the gathering dusk. He thought no one should be without a home.

Capt. Albern's dinner included a liberal portion of treacle tart. The Cook carefully laid the dishes on the chart table and hovered. Capt. Albern glanced at his favourite meal and looked at The Cook.

'The answer is no,' he said.

'No to what?' asked The Cook innocently.

'We're not giving the stowaway a berth.'

'I was just wondering.'

'Anyway, I'd have thought he'd caused you enough trouble already.'

'Trouble, Skipper?' asked The Cook, looking about in perplexed amazement.

'Letting him run up the rigging.'

'Oh that!'

'Yes that! I do cast an eye over the ship from time to time.'

'Of course, Skipper. I'll leave you to your meal.'

'Thank you.'

Capt. Albern began to eat and The Cook watched. The sea otter sighed and laid his knife and fork aside.

'He's too young for a long voyage.'

'I was thinking,' said The Cook. 'Do you remember when you gave me a berth?'

'Valparaiso. I was provisioning for a passage to Liverpool.'

'And why did you take me on?'

Capt. Albern studied his plate. 'Probably needed an extra hand,' he grunted.

'You gave me a berth because I had nowhere to lay my head. Stowaway or not, Misty would give him a home, as she has me.'

There was silence in the cabin but for the reassuring creak of the table as Misty butted into increasing seas. The night would be chilly with blustery showers, and on shore the streets would be empty and silent but for the gurgle of rain in gutters. Misty's bunks were warm and dry.

Capt. Albern sighed again, and lifted his head. 'He'll be your responsibility,' he said.

The Cook found Merrie convulsed in a fit of coughing after begging a puff of Waff's pipe.

'How would you like to be the ship's steward?' he asked.

Merrie leaped to his feet whooping with delight. 'I'll be the best steward ever!' he promised, and ran the length of the ship informing everyone he was now a sailor.

Ancell was pleased they were not stopping to put the stowaway ashore. At last he was journeying south, but there was a limit to how long whoever was calling him could hope for help. He prayed he would arrive in time.

CHAPTER 5

Misty met the swell of the Atlantic and her crew settled to the routine of a ship at sea. Helped along by the northeast trade winds the going was easy, and Capt. Albern regularly relaxed in a battered deck chair on the quarterdeck conducting the score of a symphony to an imaginary orchestra. Apart from Jobey grumbling at every meal that his was the smallest portion and in turn The Cook threatening that if he complained once more he would not be served at all, contentment reigned throughout the ship. Surveying the horizon, however, Ancell was only aware that Misty was a very small boat in the middle of a very large ocean. Every morning he climbed on deck the circle of water about the ship was unchanged and he felt a growing misgiving that they were lost.

'Are we making good progress?' he asked Chad one sunny afternoon, seeking assurance that they were well on their way.

Chad laughed. 'Ask me in a month's time. The skipper reckons we'll be in the doldrums within twenty-four hours.'

'What are the doldrums?'

'A windless area – that's when we'll have to start working,' replied the bosun, and strode off whistling cheerfully.

The following morning proved Capt. Albern right when the friendly trade winds fell away to leave Misty wallowing uncomfortably in confused seas. Her sails complained noisily, slatting against the masts, and Waff prowled the deck wincing at the wear on his canvas. For seven days the crew laboured beneath a blazing sun to keep her moving, as time and again they were called to haul on the yards and trim the sails to every fickle breath of air. They counted any sleep a luxury, by day sweating below out of the burning sun, and at night escaping the stifling heat of their bunks in the fo'c'sle to slumber uneasily on deck.

Sometimes the sky turned black, soaking them with sharp showers. Sometimes it mysteriously rained out of the blue. Occasionally a catspaw of breeze rippled the water, only to die and leave Misty rolling on the oily swell, and all the while Ancell grew more fearful, certain the ship would lay becalmed for eternity, manned by a crew of staring skeletons.

On the eighth morning he awoke to an unnatural silence. He could hear no sound of footsteps, nor even the familiar creak of Misty's rigging. The ship lay perfectly still, as if abandoned. He rushed on deck and gazed about in a panic. Not a ripple broke the surface of the sea that lay motionless to the saucer rim of the horizon, and not a breath of air stirred the lifeless sails. Capt. Albern and Truegard stood unmoving by the wheel, still waiting for a wind. He could wait no longer.

'We can't go on! Turn back!' he demanded.

Capt. Albern contained his anger. 'I am master of this ship. And what about the voice that calls you south?'

'I was mistaken.'

'I think not. I warned you it would not be easy.'

'We'll die!' screamed Ancell, and in a fury made a grab for the wheel. 'Give me a wind! Give me a wind to anywhere!' he sobbed.

Truegard wrestled him to his cabin. 'When are you going to learn to trust us?' he demanded.

'We could be becalmed forever.'

'The skipper will see us through.'

'You trust him don't you?'

'With my life,' said Truegard.

'I know I have a purpose to fulfil, but the truth is I'm not up to it.'

'Never give up. Stick to your quest, and remember the skipper took you on board because he believes in you.'

Ancell felt calmer in the presence of Truegard. He climbed the companionway and faced Capt. Albern.

'I'm sorry. You must regret giving me a berth,' he muttered.

'Never let go of your dream,' replied the sea otter.

At that moment Misty's sails flapped. Her crew looked up, holding their breath. The breeze strengthened, and with a chuckle of water at her bow Misty picked up speed. For two days the magical wind held steady, and, relieved of the labours of the calms, the sailors caught up with lost sleep and settled to their watches. Only Capt. Albern seemed uneasy as he paced the quarterdeck sniffing the air.

'I don't like it! This is a false wind,' he said to Truegard.

'Strange that it's coming out of the north when we should be picking up the south-easterlies,' agreed the first mate. Standing nearby, Ancell thought he didn't care where the wind came from provided it blew them somewhere.

'Land ahoy!' shouted Merrie from the crowsnest, to which he now climbed without a qualm.

Chips laughed. 'You'd better furl the sails then,' he called.

'It's true! I can see it!'

'You want to bet on it?' yelled Pickle, but Merrie was already scrambling down the ratlines.

'Mr Truegard, Sir,' he panted, 'I can see land.'

Truegard stooped to face the harvest mouse, ignoring the direction he was pointing.

'It will be many a day before we see land. Sometimes at sea your eyes can play tricks on you. You must learn to distinguish things that are there for what they are.'

Impatient of Truegard's lecture, Merrie ran in search of Tam and Thom relaxing below.

'I've seen an island and nobody believes me!'

'No islands here,' said Thom, and lay back on her bunk.

'Please! You must come!'

Tam sighed. 'You or me?' he said to Thom.

'You,' said Thom, and closed her eyes.

Tam followed Merrie aloft. 'I should lash you to the yardarm for disturbing my rest,' he grumbled. 'I suppose this island of yours has coconut trees - and I've told you before not to climb so fast.'

Merrie jabbed at the horizon. Tam stared and climbed higher. Thom joined Merrie.

'Tam's seen something hasn't he?'

'I saw it first!'

Thom climbed to Tam.

'Odd!' said Tam.

'Tell the skipper,' said Thom.

Truegard insisted seeing for himself before striding to the captain's cabin.

'Skipper - we've sighted an island, dead ahead.'

Capt. Albern looked up in disbelief.

'Maybe it's uncharted,' suggested Truegard.

'Unlikely, as you well know.'

Truegard frowned. 'Strange we first get a wind blowing in the wrong direction and now an island appears out of nowhere.'

'We'll have a look, but stay well clear,' said the captain. 'The sooner we pick up a true wind and get south of here the better.'

News of the island spread fast on account of Merrie informing everyone of his discovery. Ancell joined the crew lining the rail. He felt he deserved some credit for virtually summoning the wind that carried them to such an unexpected landfall. He sniffed the air, already sweet with the scent of flowers and the aroma of exotic spices. Seaweed floated by, and, to Merrie's delight, coconut shells. Slowly the island rose above the horizon – first a dark green hill of luxuriant vegetation, then black cliffs falling sheer to the sea foaming on the rocks below. Capt. Albern focused his telescope.

'No question of landing,' he informed Truegard with relief.

Truegard put the telescope to his eye. From beneath the protection of a headland, a bay of silver sand was opening into view. Calm clear water lapped a shore fringed with flowering shrubs. A waterfall splashed, throwing up a rainbow of colours, and beneath a grove of palms nestled a circle of log huts. He handed back the telescope.

'You'd better take another look,' he said.

The sea otter looked and deliberated. An apparently perfectly safe anchorage lay before them, with the opportunity to take on fresh water and possibly fresh fruit and vegetables. It would be hard on the crew to pass by. With an uneasy heart he gave the order to sail in and put a boat ashore.

CHAPTER 6

Tam rowed Truegard and The Cook shoreward - Truegard to establish friendly relations with the islanders, and The Cook to see what fresh produce might be available.

'I'm sure they'll be welcoming, but stay here,' ordered Truegard, as the gig grounded gently on the sand. 'If there's any sign of trouble get yourselves back on board - if necessary without me.'

Tam unshipped the oars and watched the first mate cross the deserted beach. He had nearly reached the huts when a powerfully built grey squirrel emerged from the jungle. At his signal, a group of rats, every one of them double the weight of Chad, quietly rose from the undergrowth. Tam fidgeted, undecided whether to obey orders or go in support of Truegard, who, tall though he was, looked slight and vulnerable compared to the island animals.

The grey squirrel stepped forward, taking careful measure of the red squirrel.

'Welcome to Careless Island,' he said.

Truegard relaxed and beckoned Tam and The Cook.

'Thank you, Sir,' he replied. ' My name is Truegard, first mate of "Misty Dawn" you see there in the bay. We ask permission to take on fresh water and provisions, though we have little to offer in return.'

The grey squirrel eyed Misty. 'Water and food we have in plenty. Your presence will be sufficient payment. My name is Larren and I rule here.' He nodded a welcome to Tam, but ignored The Cook with a flicker of distaste.

Truegard would have preferred to load the water before nightfall, but Larren insisted work should wait for the following day. First, the captain and the entire crew were to dine with him that evening - the islanders would be insulted if the sailors declined. His request frustrated, Truegard asked that at least he be shown the path to the waterfall to assess the difficulty of rolling the casks to the ship.

Larren shrugged and led the way. Crowding about the sailors, the silent rats separated The Cook from Truegard and Tam as they climbed the narrow track. The Cook, following immediately behind the long striding grey squirrel, struggled to keep up, the rats jostling and sniggering about him. One, aping his shambling gait, tripped him, causing him to stumble into Larren, who twisted away in disgust. Trembling with anger, the grey squirrel summoned a large rat to his side.

'Keep that miserable cripple away from me,' he hissed.

The waterfall splashed into a crystal clear pool. The Cook found his way barred as Truegard and Tam stepped forward to drink.

'As sweet as I've ever tasted,' announced Truegard.

'Yours for the taking tomorrow,' said Larren.

Waiting anxiously on board, the crew greeted Truegard's report of an invitation to dinner as well as a supply of fresh water and food with excitement. Capt. Albern was inclined to stay on board his ship, but accepted Truegard's argument that to do so could offend their hosts. He was adamant, however, that Misty should not be left unattended, irrespective of whether the entire crew were expected. Thom volunteered to keep watch, knowing that Tam would return with a selection of the choicest dishes for her.

'So it's called Careless Island,' said Capt. Albern.

Truegard nodded. 'So they say, and they certainly seem to have no cares.'

'More like careless to land there. I'm staying on board,' retorted The Cook.

'But we were all made welcome,' protested Truegard.

'It's no place for me,' said The Cook, and nothing Truegard said could persuade him otherwise.

The launch was lowered in the last of the short tropical twilight, and the island lay in darkness by the time they rowed ashore. On the beach the leaping flames of a fire illuminated shadowy figures loading tables with platters of food. Ancell thought it appropriate to seat himself next to the island's leader, intending to tell him of the wind he had summoned to carry Misty to his shore. But as Larren ignored him in favour of questioning Capt. Albern about his ship and crew, he satisfied himself by filling his stomach. The drink he thought especially good, and the more he drank the more satisfactory everything became. He caught Chad's warning eye and sloppily raised his goblet to him.

Chad surveyed the table. Tam was holding his head, and Skeet was not his normal cheerful self. Chips had stopped chattering and Waff was having difficulty lighting his pipe; Merrie was fast asleep and Pickle and Jobey dozing. He counted the number of rats, who were all in good spirits. There were ten, every one of them in good condition, and too many to fight. He also noticed there was no sign of Doc, and started to his feet. The rats on either side of him held him back.

'Too early to leave,' one said.

'Have some more wine,' suggested the other.

'Just stretching,' said Chad, and threw back his drink. The rats watched approvingly and refilled his cup.

'Your good health!' said Chad, and drained that too.

Larren, too, kept a watchful eye on Misty's crew as he recounted to Capt. Albern how the islanders had been shipwrecked due to the incompetence of the first mate. Both the first mate and the captain had been lost overboard, and he and the crew had been lucky to survive. As second mate, he had assumed command of the castaways and established order. They had salvaged what they could, and built the huts from what remained of the ship's timbers. Under his stewardship they enjoyed a comfortable life and had no wish to leave their island home.

'As you see, we are content here,' he concluded. He raised his voice.

'I have been telling the captain what a pleasant place this is.'

Capt. Albern glanced around the grinning, nodding rats, and pondered whether it was too soon to order his crew back on board without appearing discourteous. He wanted the peace of his cabin to think through Larren's story.

Doc had been particularly eager to go ashore to explore, even producing a butterfly net from his cavernous trunk with which he intended to hunt moths. As soon as they had landed he had wandered away in the dark, found a path into the trees and was quickly lost. He followed several tracks that led him deeper into the jungle, and eventually stumbled into a small clearing, where a pair of makeshift wooden crosses that bore no names marked two overgrown graves. He stood for a moment shaking his head sadly, then, catching the sound of distant voices, blundered back to the beach where he burst from the jungle into the party.

'I've found the graves of a couple of unfortunate souls,' he announced. 'Who are they?'

Larren stiffened and the rats stopped eating.

'The ship's captain and first mate,' said a rat, then bit his lip and fell silent.

'Though they were lost overboard, we managed to retrieve their bodies,' explained Larren quickly.

A rat spoke quietly in the grey squirrel's ear. Larren made a brief apology and strode to a hut where two of the largest rats were waiting. A furious whispered argument ensued.

'I told you to watch everybody, yet you allow a bumbling owl to wander about and find those graves,' hissed Larren.

'Doesn't matter! We say we take the ship now,' replied a rat.

Larren thought fast. They would seize the ship anyway, but if the owl's discovery had aroused Capt. Albern's suspicions, a new and better opportunity lay open to him.

'We wait until tomorrow,' he ordered. 'They'll need most of the crew to fetch the water. Once they're out of the way we'll take the ship - trust me!'

'And if we don't!' retorted the rat.

Larren eyed him coldly. 'You have no choice. You are a mutineer. We are all mutineers and we are bound together whether you like it or not.'

'Mutineers, but not murderers! You killed the captain and the first mate, not us,' growled the second rat. Larren turned on him, trembling with rage.

'If I hang, I swear you'll hang with me,' he snarled. 'We do as I say. We act tomorrow.'

On board Misty, The Cook relaxed in Capt. Albern's deck chair, enjoying the peace of the balmy night.

'I wish you'd stop marching about,' he complained. Thom stopped pacing the deck and stared at the shore.

'Tam's ill and wants to get back on board.'

'Probably those islanders' lousy food,' suggested The Cook, knowing Thom sensed how her brother felt.

'I'm going ashore to pick him up.'

'The skipper won't be pleased; you're meant to be on watch.'

'Just help me lower the gig.'

Thom rowed through the moonlit night and pulled the boat ashore close by the launch. In the glow of the fire she saw her brother half slumped at the table, and without a word helped him to his feet.

Larren tensed. 'Are there any more of your crew on board?' he questioned Capt. Albern. The sea otter rose to his feet.

'I think it's time we got some sleep. Thank you for a very fine meal,' he answered.

'Till tomorrow then,' said Larren. 'Fresh provisions and water tomorrow.'

Misty's crew stumbled wearily for the boats, wishing only to tumble into their bunks.

'I came ashore because Tam felt bad,' Thom explained.

'Glad you did. The sooner we get on board the better,' replied Capt. Albern.

'Must be the drink,' said Skeet, 'and I only had a few sips. I don't know how you can stand up, Chad, the way you were knocking it back.'

'Only to show them they couldn't put me under the table,' grunted the bosun.

With an effort they dragged the launch into the water.

'Where's Ancell?' asked Capt. Albern.

'That stupid hedgehog!' exclaimed Chad.

'Says he's on a mission and he can't even find his way across a beach. I'll get him.'

'I'll come with you,' said Truegard.

Capt. Albern glanced at the first mate, who was clearly in no condition to help anyone.

'You're to get in the launch,' he ordered. 'Thom, you're to wait with the gig for Chad. No more than five minutes, Chad. If you can't find him or any trouble seems likely, you're to come aboard.'

Chad found Ancell still sprawled across the table, watched by two rats. Ancell raised an arm in careless greeting.

'Hello Chad! Come and join us.'

'Get up! We're going on board.'

'I think I'll stay here.'

'You'll come aboard now! Captain's orders.'

'I'm comfortable here. Stop bossing me about, and have a drink,' mumbled Ancell, fumbling for his goblet. 'Did I ever tell you about a dream I once had?' he asked the two rats. Chad sighed, yanked the hedgehog to his feet and punched him hard in the stomach. Ancell folded with a gasp and Chad hoisted him onto his shoulder. The rats jumped to their feet and Chad wondered whether he would have to fight.

'Good night, gentlemen!' he growled, showing his teeth, and started for the gig. The rats hesitated, then stood aside, but followed a few paces behind. Chad noticed other rats slowly closing in on him. He wondered if he could make the gig if he ran, but he was encumbered with the weight of Ancell. He took a chance and span round.

'Thank you for a lovely dinner,' he called. 'See you all in the morning.'

The rats paused and stood uncertainly.

'In the morning,' said one eventually.

'Bright and early,' confirmed Chad, and strode for the boat.

Never had Capt. Albern been so relieved to step on board Misty. He surveyed his officers and crew, all of whom, with the exception of The Cook, Thom and Chad, were fighting the lethargy he felt.

The Cook dispensed mugs of strong tea. 'Serves you right for being greedy,' he told Jobey, who was slumped against a hatch, holding his head.

'The food was all right. It's those rats I worry about,' said Chad. 'We're outnumbered if it comes to a fight.'

'We were made welcome. Nobody's thinking of fighting,' said Truegard.

'Welcome or not, they're as evil a pack as I've ever seen,' retorted Chad.

Capt. Albern listened to Truegard and he listened to Chad. He pondered Larren's account of the captain and first mate lost overboard, and he considered the fresh supplies on hand the following day. Then he listened to Misty tugging at her anchor chain, pleading to sail, and made up his mind.

'Gentlemen! We sail immediately! I was mistaken to land here, and I apologise for my bad judgement.' Truegard looked surprised and the crew groaned.

'Can't we sleep first?' wailed Jobey.

'If the skipper says we're sailing, we sail. Let's get to it,' answered Truegard.

The crew laboured in a daze of fatigue. Only Chad and Thom had the energy to do much of the work, and Truegard, Skeet, The Cook and the captain had to lend their weight to the capstan to raise anchor. Slumbering on his bunk, where Chad had unceremoniously dumped him, Ancell half woke. He wondered vaguely what the commotion on deck was about, decided he did not care, and closed his eyes.

Larren listened to the clank of the anchor chain, and smiling, quickly stole through the dark to the makeshift fishing raft the islanders had built from the wrecked ship's timbers.

'So, Capt. Albern, as I suspected, you don't trust me,' he murmured, as he pushed off from the shore. 'And rightly so, for tomorrow I would have seized your ship. But all the better for me you flee in the night.'

He heard the rats run from the huts,

shouting in angry confusion at Misty's sudden departure, and glancing back, laughed. 'Farewell my mutinous friends,' he muttered. 'With you as my crew, how long before one of you betrayed me? For money perhaps? Or on your wretched deathbed to save your soul? Enjoy your island paradise, for Larren will not return to rescue you.'

CHAPTER 7

Ancell awoke with an aching head, feeling confused and angry, and wondering why Chad had unaccountably hit him and Misty was sailing. Stumbling up the companionway he asked The Cook for a mug of tea. None of the crew bade him good morning.

'All gone,' said The Cook, and turned his back.

Ancell accosted Chad. 'What's going on! And why did you hit me last night?'

'Quickest way of getting you on board. You were being stupid again.'

'What do you mean by 'again'?'

'Three times you've denied this call you say you're answering. You dither about sailing with us; as soon as we lose the wind you want to turn back, and last night you stay on the island when the skipper orders us on board. Doesn't seem the best way to follow a dream.'

'I suppose you're right,' muttered Ancell, staring at the deck. 'The truth is I'm no adventurer. I'd rather have stayed at home. It's just that I know someone needs my help.'

Chad sighed. 'If anyone needs looking after, it's you. Goodness knows what will become of you when you step off Misty.'

'Something will turn up. Meanwhile, the next time I do something stupid, hit me, but not as hard as last night; my stomach still hurts.'

Chad smiled. 'That was just a poke.'

'I still don't understand why we left so quickly.'

'The skipper felt uneasy about the place. That's a good enough reason for me, and it should be for you. If a member of the crew had delayed us last night they'd be scrubbing the deck.'

Ancell came to a decision. 'Where do I find a scrubbing brush?'

'You! You wouldn't last ten minutes.'

'Try me.'

Chad grinned. 'We'll make a sailor of you yet,' he said, and fetched a bucket.

Ancell scrubbed, the sun burning his back and his head spinning. He stuck at it for an hour, and was about to give up, when Chips complimented him on his work. He redoubled his efforts, and after another hour, Skeet stopped to chat and explain the importance of maintaining standards on a long voyage. He scrubbed on and The Cook brought him a mug of tea. He was still scrubbing when Truegard came on watch.

'What's come over Ancell?' the first mate asked Capt. Albern.

'Chad had a word with him about last night.'

'A bit hard to make him scrub the deck, Skipper.'

'He volunteered. I imagine Chad has got through to him that the moment he stepped on board he belonged to Misty. He'll feel more at home now.' Truegard watched the bosun replenish Ancell's bucket.

'Well done Chad,' he murmured.

Five days after Careless Island had dropped below the horizon, Misty picked up the trusty southeast trade winds, and with a favourable current under her, surged south. The crew settled to their watches, and Ancell made sure he helped with the menial tasks of the shipboard routine. He was rubbing down rust with Chad when Truegard stopped by. The first mate gazed up at the billowing sails. 'A few weeks and we'll be at The Cape,' he said.

Ancell vaguely remembered the charts Capt. Albern had unrolled the day he had first stepped on board Misty.

'Would that be Cape Horn?' he asked.

'The tip of South America, more than forty degrees south,' confirmed Truegard. 'We'll have to battle against the westerly winds down there to beat round it.'

'The roaring forties they're called,' added

Chad. 'That's where you'll feel some wind.' He smirked. 'If you weren't already short of a tail you'd need to hold onto it then.'

Ancell ignored him.

'And after The Cape?' he asked Truegard.

'We cross the wide Pacific to Australia,' said the first mate.

A full moon, lighting Misty's sails a ghostly white, hung low on the horizon at the midnight change of watch. Skeet, Tam and Thom retired to their bunks. Pickle took the helm, humming a sea shanty and Jobey yawned and rubbed the sleep from his eyes. Truegard gazed astern, watching the silver wake. He felt a long shadow fall across him and shivered, though the night was warm. He heard Pickle catch his breath and fall silent, and turning, took a step back as the apparition of Larren staggered towards him, looming large in the face of the moon.

'Water - give me water,' croaked the grey squirrel.

'How did you get on board?' gasped Truegard.

'Clung to the bowsprit until I saw a chance to hide in the launch,' whispered Larren.

Jobey brought a mug of water, which Larren sipped, then drained. Truegard roused Capt. Albern, but the stowaway was too weak to talk, and after devouring some biscuits and drinking again, was half carried below.

'He's a tough one; long time to last without

food or water,' commented Pickle. Capt. Albern said nothing, but paced the deck for a long while.

Larren recovered quickly, and the following morning was able to walk unaided to the captain's cabin, where he told his tale. The dreadful night of the shipwreck there had been a mutiny and the captain and first mate killed. He had pleaded with the rats to spare them, but to no avail, and was about to suffer the same fate himself when the ship drove on the rocks. Fearful of finding themselves castaways, the crew then started fighting among themselves, all blaming each other.

'I fled,' said Larren. 'But it's a small island, and a search party soon found me. If I wished to live, they said, I was to exercise my authority as second mate and restore order. And so I became the prisoner of those I command.'

Capt. Albern stroked his whiskers. 'Why did you not tell me the truth when we landed?'

'You saw how closely I was watched and every word I uttered marked. I had no hopes of escape.'

'But you did.'

'I overheard them plotting to seize your ship. I managed to slip away to warn you, but as I drew close you prepared to sail. If my absence had been discovered before I returned I would have been held to blame and certainly killed.'

'So why hide for five days? Why hide at all?' asked Capt. Albern.

'For fear of you putting me ashore.'

'In other words I might not believe your story. We can yet turn back.'

'Then you will send me to my death,' said Larren.

All morning the grey squirrel stood alone at the plunging bow. He noted with satisfaction that Misty had not changed course. Capt. Albern paced his cabin, and at the midday change of watch called Truegard, Skeet and Chad below. He repeated Larren's story.

'As you know, gentlemen, we can ill afford losing ten days taking him back,' he added.

'Unthinkable to return him lest we put his life in danger,' said Truegard. 'We should keep him safe on board and let him tell his story to the authorities when we make landfall.'

'He seems very capable, and an extra hand would be useful in the Southern Ocean,' added Skeet.

'Put him in irons,' growled Chad.

'We don't know if he's committed any crime,' argued Truegard. 'We can't condemn him out of hand.'

'I'd be inclined to lock him up if we were close to port,' said Capt. Albern, 'but holding him a prisoner day after day would demoralise the crew. He'll have to work his passage. Mr Truegard, I'd like you to take him on your watch. Keep an eye on him - and please inform the crew of my decision.'

'Personally I'd chuck him overboard,' muttered Chad to Skeet as they trooped up the companionway.

Larren kept to himself, not caring to talk about the island and ignoring Pickle's persistent questioning. He worked quietly and capably, only once flaring into anger when Chad informed him he was to share the crew's quarters in the fo'c'sle with The Cook. Chad had retorted that if he cared to sleep on deck in the bitter cold of the Southern Ocean he was welcome to it.

As the days passed, the soft blue water of the tropics hardened to the steel grey of the South Atlantic. The nights grew chill and the crew searched their sea bags for warm clothing, struggled into oilskins and drew sou'westers tightly about their heads - in Chips's case, over and above his bowler. Under Waff's watchful eye, Misty's lightweight sails were changed for heavy weather canvas as she pitched into breaking seas.

Having received little more than an occasional nod from the grey squirrel, Ancell was surprised when one evening Larren squeezed through his cabin door.

'I thought it was time we had a chat,' said Larren.

'By all means,' Ancell stammered. He was a little in awe of the stowaway who had endured hunger and thirst for so long.

'I understand you're on a quest,' said Larren.

'Sort of,' Ancell mumbled. Larren embodied all the qualities of the courageous adventurer he lacked.

'I thought there was something special about you,' continued Larren. 'I admire your resolve, and I will be glad to help you in any way I can.'

'Thank you,' replied Ancell, pleased at the compliment. 'I'm glad to have you on board.'

Larren talked of the mutiny, and of his determination to bring the perpetrators to justice.

'We've a good crew on board Misty,' said Ancell.

'By and large excellent,' agreed Larren, 'though I worry about the first mate.'

'Truegard's admired by everyone. The skipper and every single member of the crew trust him.'

'Maybe, but popularity doesn't make a good officer. I just wonder if he's up to the job if things get tough. Perhaps it's because he reminds me of the incompetent first mate on my ship who cared only for himself.'

'Truegard cares for everyone.'

'I hope you're right. At least he looks the part, which is more than can be said of that dead-beat of a bosun. I apologise! I've spoken out of turn. I hope Chad's not a friend of yours.'

'Oh no!' said Ancell quickly. 'No particular friend of mine.'

'Glad to hear it,' said Larren, and eased himself out.

Ancell shifted uneasily on his bunk. He supposed a fine creature like Larren would think Misty's bosun a little coarse, but he also felt he had let Chad down.

Reefed to less than half her canvas, Misty beat into the tumbling waste of the Southern Ocean, an old sea, cold and spiteful. Jobey glared at his dinner as he clung to the galley door to save himself being flung across the rolling deck.

'Those plates have got more than me,' he complained.

'Special for the officers,' grunted The Cook.

'I deserve anything they get.'

'It's sauerkraut. You won't like it.'

'If they have it, so should I.'

The Cook sighed and spooned a large portion onto Jobey's plate.

'I'll have some too,' demanded Pickle.

'It tastes awful,' spluttered Jobey.

'I said you wouldn't like it. I told you it was more to the taste of officers,' confirmed The Cook.

'My taste is as good as theirs,' declared Jobey, and forced it down.

The Cook handed Merrie a plate to take to the captain's cabin.

'Don't drop it, and hold on when you move. We don't want you going overboard,' he instructed. Merrie slithered along the deck and delivered the meal intact. Capt. Albern poked a fork at the sauerkraut.

'Do you know what this is?' he said.

'I can't remember the name Sir, but I could ask The Cook for you,' offered Merrie helpfully.

'It helps keep you healthy when we're out of fresh provisions. Make sure you eat yours.'

'The Cook said it was for the officers.'

'It's just his way of encouraging everyone to eat something they may not like,' replied the captain. 'If he told them it was good for them they'd probably throw it overboard. Remember to hold on when you go back.'

'Yes, Sir,' said Merrie, and promptly attempted to return with his arms outstretched, immediately to be pitched across the deck. Thom hauled him to his feet.

'You could have gone over the side,' she warned. 'You must remember to…'

'I know! I know!' interrupted Merrie as he limped back to the galley nursing a bruised shoulder and a painful shin.

Misty drove further south. The wind turned icy, and the duty watches stamped their feet and threw their arms about their chests, willing the time away until they could crawl into the warmth of their bunks. Ancell and Doc spent much of their time in the relative comfort of their cabins, Doc engrossed in his books, and Ancell wondering if Misty would soon sail off the bottom of the world.

'How long to the end of our watch?' Pickle asked Truegard, one early evening as he shivered at the helm.

'Half an hour, but I want the fore topsail furled before you go below.'

'Can't it wait. Tam and Thom will be able to cope,' pleaded Jobey.

'I think it may blow up a little. Better to make her comfortable for the night, and better to do it when they come on watch. I'll let them sleep until then.'

'But it will take an hour - an hour of my sleep!'

'I'm sure Mr Skeet would do the same for you,' said Truegard.

Larren listened, but said nothing.

It was hard and tiring work securing the thrashing canvas to the wildly swaying yard, and it was nearly dark before the two watches climbed down to the deck. Skeet, Tam and Thom commenced their duty, and Pickle, Jobey and Larren hurried below to at last pull off their oilskins.

'Now I'm colder than ever!' grumbled Jobey,

'and I thought it was going to be an easy watch.'

'But on the bright side, at least we won't be hauled on deck as soon as we get our heads down,' replied Pickle, climbing into his bunk.

'It was poor judgement,' interrupted Larren. 'It's a weak first mate who dithers. He should have got the sail in earlier when there was plenty of light. He put us all at an unnecessary risk.'

Jobey kicked off his sea boots and advanced on the grey squirrel. He stood no higher than Larren's chest.

'You watch it!' he pronounced, jabbing Larren in the stomach. Larren took a step back.

'I was merely agreeing with one of your perfectly justifiable complaints,' he muttered.

'Well don't!' seethed Jobey, continuing to prod. 'I'll have you know Truegard chose me to be on his watch. It's my right to grumble if I want to. That doesn't mean you can criticise. Truegard's the best.'

'Fine! If that's what you want to believe,' retorted Larren. 'Personally I'd like to see your gentlemanly first mate pull his weight a bit more.'

'Shut up, and go to sleep,' said Pickle.

Larren did not sleep, but considered his likely fate. He had been on board Misty long enough to realise Capt. Albern would hand him over to the authorities the moment Misty made port. Also his hopes of causing dissention among the crew, engineering a mutiny, and taking command were fading by the day. He had quickly recognised he could never isolate the captain from his first mate; the bond between them was as father and son. Truegard would never forsake Misty's master. But he was also failing to turn the crew against Truegard, whom they trusted without reservation. He thought it ironic that the red squirrel who thwarted his plans should be the one who treated him most kindly, and he hated him all the more for it. He consoled himself that Misty had yet many thousands of miles to sail. He would have to bide his time.

Ancell was awoken early one morning by a thorough shaking from Doc.

'Get up, you lazy animal! Come and have a look!' urged the owl, and hurried up the companionway. Ancell groaned and followed. Misty barely heeled to a gentle breeze, the sea had moderated to a long swell, and abeam the cliffs of Cape Horn stood stark in the watery light of the dawn.

'I wish we'd sail nearer, I'd like to take a closer look,' said Doc. Ancell watched the white surf surging onto the jagged rocks and shivered.

'This is close enough for me,' he said.

In his cabin, Capt. Albern stared hard at the barometer and redrew a line on the chart, taking

Misty ever further south. He climbed on deck and gave Skeet the new course.

'Not turning west yet, Skipper?' asked Skeet. Capt. Albern motioned at the rocky headland.

'Can't risk being driven back on that lot. I'm afraid we're in for a blow. I've never seen the glass fall so quickly.' Skeet looked up at the clear sky and surveyed the placid sea.

'I've never known you wrong, Skipper, but I bet that in twenty-four hours we'll be round and safely on our way.'

'I wish you were right, Mr Skeet, but I fear the twenty-four hours you need we lost by landing at Careless Island and it will cost us dear.'

Ancell overheard and uneasily remembered praying for the wind that carried them to the isle. He also recalled it was he who had delayed their departure.

Throughout the morning the crew prepared Misty to meet the storm. Capt. Albern ordered double lashings on the launch, the gig and the anchor. Below deck, anything that could move was made secure, and in the galley The Cook stowed everything but the bare essentials.

At midday The Cook served a meal of such generous portions, Jobey was lost for words. In the afternoon Capt. Albern suspended Chad's endless routine of chores and ordered the crew to get as much sleep as possible. Throughout the night Misty sailed serenely deeper southward, her progress falling away when the clement breeze died, abandoning her to await what the Southern Ocean held in store.

At dawn, Capt. Albern looked at the sky, looked at the sea and sniffed the air.

'I'm afraid you've lost your bet, Mr Skeet,' he said, and gave the order to reduce Misty's canvas to storm sails only.

'Your captain's mad,' Larren told Waff as they lowered the mainsail. 'No wind, and he reduces sail! If it's going to blow, why doesn't he wait until it does.'

'Just get the sail down and secure it well,' grunted Waff. 'The skipper knows what he's doing, and you'll soon find out why.'

CHAPTER 8

The storm hit Misty hard from the beginning, the weight of the wind laying her on her side and whipping the long swell into walls of fast moving water, their breaking crests determined to turn the ship over and smash her to pieces in a welter of seething surf. Curtains of hard stinging rain closed the horizon and lashed the sailors, forcing them to bend low to protect their eyes.

Pitched across the deck, Ancell clung to the rail, barely able to see or breathe.

'Get below!' yelled Chad. 'This is just the start.'

Hour by hour the wind and sea raged at the little ship and hour after hour Capt. Albern stood by the helm, unbending and steadfast, his piercing blue eyes searching for a passage through the savage waste of waters. Huddled below, Merrie and The Cook listened to the murderous brutality of the Southern Ocean and felt Misty's timbers shiver as tons of tumbling water swept her decks.

'Are we going to sink?' yelled Merrie, firmly

crooked in The Cook's good arm. The Cook wondered if any ship could survive such a hammering.

'The skipper will see us through. Sleep if you can,' he shouted.

But sleep was impossible as Misty pitched, rolled, kicked and bucked as she fought the tempest, bravely climbing to the crest of every wave, then with a sickening lurch, her masts wildly clawing at the sky, plunging to the trough below. Icy water swilled about Ancell's cabin. Wedging himself into his bunk, numb with fear and shivering with cold, he tried to stop his ears to the roaring wrath of the ocean and the moan of the wind that rose to a howl, and then a shriek of venom as it tore at Misty's rigging. The twenty-four hours he had lost Misty weighed on his conscience. He felt only a sadness that he should die, his quest unfulfilled, but an overwhelming remorse that he had cost Capt. Albern and his crew their lives. Certain that Misty would founder, he clawed his way to the top of the companionway, where he lay waiting for the end.

Night chased out the last vestiges of light and swallowed Misty in a primeval wailing darkness. At midnight, Truegard handed the helm to Larren, but sensing the storm was nearing its peak, declined Capt. Albern's instruction to rest below and remained at his skipper's side. As Larren took the wheel the tempest intensified to a crescendo of violence. Out of the darkness the wind bayed at the grey squirrel, and in the darkness Larren's face twisted with fury, his curses whipped into the raging night.

'Damn you wind and damn you wave,' he screamed. 'You'll not take me nor this ship I'll one day make my own. I'll see you in hell before you master Larren.'

Straining through the dark, Capt. Albern glimpsed the crest of a mountain of water bearing down on the ship – a wave riding on the back of another and rearing to the height of Misty's masts. He saw Larren steer directly at the breaking sea, perversely pitting the ship against the worst the elements could muster, and sprang to wrestle the wheel from the grey squirrel. Misty immediately lurched violently, leaving her master clinging to the helm and throwing Larren half overboard.

Ancell watched Capt. Albern control the wheel as Misty began to climb the advancing wall of water. Then he saw Truegard fling himself across the deck to grasp the struggling grey squirrel, only to stagger at a kick to his face and lie stunned and in danger of being washed over the side. Sobbing in desperation, he began to crawl towards the first mate as Larren clambered to safety. Waving him back, Capt.

Albern spun the wheel, Misty rolled sharply, and Truegard was thrown back to be caught and held by his skipper.

With a firm grip on his first mate, the sea otter steadied Misty as she climbed more steeply. She faltered as the foaming crest reared above her, her masts tracing wild arcs heavenward, crying for help. Her master summoned all his will, and agonisingly slowly she responded to breast the peak and corkscrew over, all the strength gone out of her.

Ordered to rest below, the crew tensed and held their breath as Misty climbed, then breathed again as the wave broke into a thunderous cauldron of seething white water behind her. Then they heard the pistol shot crack of the fore-spencer sail ripping and in seconds tearing into flogging tatters of canvas. Without sufficient sail to face the storm Misty laid broadside on and at her most vulnerable to the seas that were bent on her destruction.

'We'll have to wear her round and run with the wind,' yelled Capt. Albern to Truegard.

Truegard pointed to the foremast, where the heavy wooden gaff, freed by the torn sail, was slamming into the rigging.

'Got to get it down!' he shouted.

'Too dangerous in the dark,' answered the captain. 'We'll see what Waff can do at first light. I think the worst is over.'

For long tense minutes Misty lay at a frightening angle, one side of her deck beneath the surging water as her master nursed her round. At last she shook herself free, and with the wind behind her, fled eastward.

'Get some rest!' Capt. Albern ordered Truegard. 'I'll take her until dawn.'

Truegard crawled for'ard and recognised Chad and Waff staring up the foremast.

'The gaff's jammed. Got to make it fast,' yelled Chad.

'The skipper says we're to wait until first light,' shouted Truegard.

Waff shook his head. 'Must do it now! It'll bring the mast down.'

Truegard doubted whether even Waff, the surest of all the crew aloft, could work in such conditions. The bulk of Chips appeared out of the darkness. Waff turned on him.

'You're in the way. Get back below before you go overboard!'

'Not until you do, you old fool,' shouted Chips.

'Make yourself useful then and haul me up,' demanded Waff.

With infinite care, the polecat was hoisted up the wildly reeling mast. Truegard and Chad peered up into the dark, teeth clenched and saying nothing. Head bowed, Chips muttered what a stubborn, perverse and bloody-minded animal Waff was, who deserved to be flung to his death, and prayed to see him come down safe. Twenty minutes passed before the job was done and the bruised and exhausted sailmaker lowered to the deck. Chad and Chips half carried him below and laid him on his bunk.

'I reckon you've just saved us a lot of trouble,' said Chad.

'I don't know what took you so long! Were you having a quiet pipe up there?' said Chips.

Waff glared at him, but passed out before he could snort a reply.

Throughout the night Capt. Albern kept vigil with his stricken ship, and at dawn, The Cook miraculously produced hot drinks. Ancell was shivering so much he could barely raise the mug to his lips. Chad steadied his arm.

'Don't waste it! It will warm you up.'

'Will we sink?'

'The skipper has never lost a ship.'

'I don't know how he can stay on deck for so long. I'm so cold I can't think.'

'A million waterproof hairs a square inch helps – better than that bunch of spines of yours. Anyway you've enough fat on you to keep you going.'

'I'm not fat!'

'Well rounded then.'

Ancell eyed the state of Chad. 'Now I know what a drowned rat looks like,' he said.

For three long days and nights the storm drove Misty eastward before abandoning her to wallow in its wake, careless of whether she lived or died. Day after day the crew manned the pumps and baled out bucket after bucket of icy water from the fo'c'sle. When they could rest they crawled into their sodden bunks, teeth chattering and aching with exhaustion. On the fourth morning they savoured steaming hot bowls of porridge for breakfast and The Cook was the hero of the hour. Capt. Albern inspected the worst of the leaks below and surveyed the scars of the battle on deck. He called Truegard, Skeet, Chad and The Cook to his cabin and pointed to a pencilled cross on the chart.

'Our position, Gentleman,' he reported. There was a solemn hush - Misty had been driven back four hundred miles.

'Any of the crew injured?' he asked.

Truegard and Skeet reported nothing serious apart from the badly bruised sailmaker.

'Provisions?' he enquired.

'Nine weeks, if we start rationing now,' replied The Cook.

'We've suffered too much damage to attempt The Horn again,' said the captain, 'so if we can't make Australia going west, we'll go east.'

'All the way across the Indian Ocean, Skipper?' queried Skeet. 'How long will it take?'

'Nine weeks - if we're lucky,' said the

captain, and ushered them out. Truegard was the last to leave and Capt. Albern motioned him to take a seat. Truegard watched the sea otter, drawn and grey with fatigue, carefully stretch and sit back, humming a tune and seemingly content – even triumphant. For a while they sat in easy silence.

'Well! What do you think?' said the captain.

Instinctively Truegard understood what was on his skipper's mind.

'We survived,' he observed.

'Exactly! And no one lost. I count it a victory. How's Ancell?'

'A few bruises and convinced we would founder. Also rambling a bit – something about the wind that carried us to Careless Island and our present plight being his fault.'

'He may be right on both counts. Even so our task is to see he holds onto his dream. And what of Larren?'

'Angry that you took the wheel from him.'

'Misty was uneasy with him at the helm. Take care, Truegard, take care.'

Truegard studied the chart in silence. 'And now for good or ill we are driven east. I pray no more will be demanded of us,' he murmured half to himself.

'We don't control the elements,' replied the sea otter, rising wearily. 'Time we all got some sleep. Have the crew rest as much as possible today, and tomorrow we'll start on the repairs. And ask The Cook to serve a tot of rum all round.'

Truegard rose to leave.

'There's just one more thing,' said the sea otter. 'You remember I said I especially needed you on this voyage?' He hesitated; then looked up at the red squirrel. 'I just want you to know I'm glad you're at my side.'

Truegard smiled. 'Where else would I be,' he said.

A hot dinner inside him, and warmed by the rum, Ancell watched the last ragged fragments of cloud chase above Misty's swaying masts. The blood red setting sun towards which they had sailed, now dipped below the storm tossed horizon behind them.

'How close is Australia this way?' he asked Truegard and Chad.

'About seven thousand miles close,' said Chad with a grin. 'I guarantee you'll be a slimmer hedgehog by the time we step ashore.'

'I have to get there.'

'Those mysterious voices still calling you? Perhaps you'd ask them where I can get a warm dry bed for the night.'

'You don't understand.'

'The skipper does,' said Truegard, 'which is why he's determined to see you to wherever you are destined to go.'

Day after day the crew worked on the damage

to the ship. Chips toiled from dawn to dusk, shoring up the sprung planking and rebuilding the splintered gig. Tam and Thom worked aloft for hours on end, making good the weakened rigging. Truegard and Skeet left their posts at the helm to help. Waff moved slowly and painfully, and Chad allocated Ancell to work with him.

'If you sit on the deck you can't fall over,' he instructed, 'and remember not to curl up or you'll roll overboard.'

'I sometimes wish you'd roll up!' called Ancell, as the bosun scrambled up the rigging to replace a broken block.

'And no dreaming!' yelled back Chad.

Under Waff's watchful eye, Ancell set about cutting spare canvas into strips to caulk Misty's hull, which Jobey delivered to Truegard, who lay on his back in the bowels of the ship, soaked in icy water, painstakingly sealing the leaking timbers.

'I'll do the next one,' Jobey offered.

'No point in you getting frozen as well,' grunted Truegard. 'Pump her out again, and we'll see how dry she stays.'

Jobey hurried to the pumps, grabbing Pickle on the way.

'Get pumping,' he ordered.

'Captain Jobey now is it!' retorted Pickle.

'Truegard is working in the bilges half under water.'

'Why didn't you say so,' said Pickle, and together they pumped hard.

Capt. Albern nursed Misty a little to the north of east for calmer waters, and night after night took long spells at the helm while the weary crew slept. At meal times he took his place in the queue of hungry sailors waiting for The Cook to dole half portions on their plates.

'I'm still hungry,' announced Merrie.

'You're eating too quickly. Make it last,' said Truegard, and slipped him a spoonful of his meagre meal.

'Thanks!' said Merrie, and swallowed it in a mouthful.

Larren watched, despising the first mate's small act of kindness. He thought it was typical of the red squirrel, whose calm assurance had united the crew in the battle to save their ship, and now sustained their resolve to face their adversities without complaint. He remembered Truegard coming to his aid at the height of the storm, and shrugged imperceptibly. The storm, he thought, had served him well. The closer the crew came to starvation the more susceptible they would become to suggestions of rebellion. He could count on the weak hedgehog, not that he was of any consequence. Only Truegard stood in his way, but from the moment the red squirrel had saved his life, he knew what he would do.

CHAPTER 9

"Completed all repairs possible at sea," wrote Capt. Albern in the ship's log on the tenth morning after the storm. Under jury rig, carrying what canvas she could on her damaged spars, Misty ploughed her lonely course across the vastness of an ocean that circled half the globe.

Doc worked on Pickle's guitar, snapped at the neck, despite being carefully stowed. The owl had insisted on helping with every repair. But after falling over and knocking Chips from his work bench; becoming so entangled in a coil of rope that Tam had just untangled that it took both Tam and Thom to extricate him, and getting stuck in the hatch while endeavouring to carry wet bedding on deck to air, he had been informed by Chad that he was more likely to sink the ship than save it, and banished to his cabin. He presented his handiwork to Pickle.

'Where's my guitar?' said Pickle.

'I've made a few design improvements,' explained Doc.

Pickle studied what had once looked like a guitar, plucked a string, and winced.

'It just needs tuning a bit,' Doc advised, 'then you can strum to your hearts content.'

'Spare us that!' groaned Jobey.

Merrie rushed towards them.

'Doc! Chips is hurt! You've got to come quick!' he begged.

Doc hurried to where Chips lay. The carpenter had allowed a chisel to slip and gashed his leg. Chad knelt at his side trying to stem the flow of blood creeping across the deck. Doc peered, put on his pince-nez, looked closer, and fainted.

'Get Waff, he'll know what to do,' groaned Chips.

The sailmaker arrived armed with a tin box of assorted needles and twine. He looked at the leg and sighed.

'It'll have to come off!' he stated.

'Thought so,' agreed Chad, looking grave.

'Quit fooling and do something,' protested Chips.

The Cook handed the carpenter a tot of rum and stared at the wound. 'I'll get my meat cleaver,' he said.

'Will someone please do something before I bleed to death,' pleaded Chips.

Waff threaded a needle. 'Stop complaining – it just needs a few stitches,' he said, and settling himself on Doc's ample stomach, began to sew.

Chips yelled. In a flash Chad whipped off the carpenter's bowler.

'Give it back!' begged Chips.

'It's all wet. It'll give you pneumonia. I think I'll throw it overboard,' shouted Chad, capering about the deck.

'Give me my hat!' railed Chips, craning his neck to follow the fate of his beloved bowler. Chad restored it to his head, but not before Waff had sewn the last stitch.

'All done!' announced the polecat, nimbly dressing the wound. 'I recommend no talking for three months to help it heal.'

'I hope you made a better job of it than your sails!' flung the beaver after the departing sailmaker.

'What happened?' Doc asked Chad, climbing unsteadily to his feet.

'You fainted.'

'Ah yes! All that blood, can't stand the sight of it!'

'But you're a doctor!'

'Indeed I am - Eugene Beaufoy, Doctor of Philosophy. A discipline, may I inform you, of universal importance.'

'But not a lot of use for first aid,' Chad retorted.

Chips hobbled for a few days, and Pickle spent six weeks restoring his guitar to its original shape whilst Misty limped east, her weary crew weakening with hunger every passing watch. Only Truegard's unshakeable faith that they would make landfall sustained their will to survive. And all the while Larren plotted.

At last the West Australian current swept the ship north. The skies cleared and the sun warmed their emaciated bodies.

'How long before we arrive in port?' Ancell asked Truegard, as Misty ghosted through a moonless night.

'We're not capable of making a port. The best we can hope for is a sandy shore to put her aground.'

'But how long?'

'Within seven days.'

'And then a good meal,' said Pickle.

'I bet we arrive just after the shops shut,' prophesied Jobey.

Truegard laughed. 'Much of the coast is deserted, apart from which, we first have to get ashore, which will be risky.'

'Well there you are!' Jobey told Pickle. 'You can choose whether to drown or starve.'

Thinking more of his stomach than the problems of beaching a ship, Ancell bade the watch good night.

Larren stood alone at the bow. Night by night he had watched the moon wane until not a glimmer of light reflected on the ship. He stole aft through the dark.

'The bobstay may be working loose. I think you should have a look,' he told Truegard.

Truegard paled. If the chain securing the bowsprit failed, the foremast could collapse at any moment and with it any chance of the ship making land. For a brief moment he hesitated – climbing onto the bowsprit in the dark was dangerous and he suddenly feared for his life. But if he delayed until daylight the entire ship's company might perish. For their sakes he had to face the task. Reluctantly he followed the grey squirrel for'ard into the dark, and climbing out onto the bowsprit leaned over to feel for the damage.

'Everything seems firm enough. We'll check it in the morning,' he said.

'Then look closer,' whispered Larren, and kicked hard.

Stunned by the blow, arms outstretched, Truegard hit the ice-cold water and knew no more. Larren leaned on the rail, breathing hard and counting the minutes – then composing himself ran aft.

'Truegard's slipped and gone overboard!' he cried. He rushed for'ard again.

'All hands on deck!' he screamed down the fore hatch.

Capt. Albern appeared before a single member of the crew had moved.

'It's Mr Truegard, Sir,' whispered Pickle.

Ashen faced, Capt. Albern issued a string of orders to bring Misty about and retrace her course. Never had her crew worked so fast. All night they searched, back and fourth, time and time again, straining through the dark for sight or sound of the gentle red squirrel.

'We will find him, won't we?' sobbed Merrie.

The Cook turned away, wiping his own tears, unable to reply. He knew, as did Chad and Waff scanning the dark waters from aloft, as did Tam and Thom, who took the responsibility at the helm, and as did Skeet, Chips, Jobey and Pickle, peering into the night, that the task was hopeless. Yet they searched on, disbelief that they would never see their beloved Truegard again overtaken by an aching sense of loss. Other than Capt. Albern's whispered orders to turn and search and turn again, not a word was spoken. Ancell stood with Doc. He looked to speak to Skeet, saw the tears falling, and said nothing. All night, Capt. Albern stood alone at the stern, staring into the dark, his eyes shadowed with grief, too heart-broken for the tears to fall - and at the bow Larren practiced the account he would give of the accident.

Tentative fingers of light filtered from beneath the eastern horizon, reluctant to unveil the sorrowful ship and light the joyless day. Again and again the distraught captain uttered a barely audible order to turn about and search again. At mid-day, The Cook quietly left his post and brewed a kettle of tea, and Chad and Waff climbed down the ratlines to signal the end of what from the beginning had been but a forlorn hope.

Skeet's heart sank when The Cook handed him a mug for Capt. Albern. Bereft of Truegard's advice, he was at a loss of how to approach or what to say to the sea otter.

'I'll take it,' offered Chad.

Capt. Albern stood gazing at the horizon, rooted to Misty's deck as if destined to search for his beloved first mate for eternity. Chad silently offered the tea. The sea otter motioned it aside.

'To what purpose are the best sacrificed,' he whispered.

Chad said nothing, wondering at the words of his grief stricken skipper. Again he held out the mug. Capt. Albern drew a deep breath.

'Please ask Mr Skeet to resume our course,' he said.

Misty crept east, as if ashamed to cease to search. The crew moved mechanically, speaking little, and many a time each of them paused from their work, distracted by thoughts of the red squirrel who had meant so much to them. Larren kept to himself, relieved that Capt. Albern had neither summoned him nor held an enquiry into the fate of the first mate. It seemed the sea otter cared nothing for the circumstances of Truegard's death, but only that the red squirrel would never again stand at his side.

For five days Ancell watched the captain attend to his duties in a trance, numb with pain, unapproachable and inconsolable. On the sixth morning he tapped at the sea otter's cabin door.

'It's me, Ancell,' he ventured.

Slumped over the chart table, Capt. Albern raised his haggard face. Ancell looked into the blue eyes clouded with sorrow.

'You must not give in. Truegard will always be with you,' he blurted.

'And what of you and your quest?' asked the captain.

'I know I've wavered before, but never again. For as long as I remember Truegard I'll not forsake him. That I promise you.'

'Then we go on,' Capt. Albern replied.

The following day Misty's crew watched cumulous cloud build on the horizon before them.

'There's your Australia, under that cloud. We'll make landfall tomorrow,' Chad told Ancell.

Misty slipped through the night, and at first light her crew climbed the rigging to stare at a low, arid coastline. Calm waters lapped sandy beaches, protected by a reef a few hundred yards from the shore, where the long swell built and broke in a line of white surf. High in the crowsnest, Thom searched for a gap into the tranquil water. She spied a break and pointed.

'It's very small,' she called.

Capt. Albern climbed the ratlines, looked long and hard at the narrow strip of blue that offered Misty a chance of beaching safely, and coaxed his weary ship towards the entrance.

Ancell listened to the boom of the breakers surging onto the coral that would rip the bottom out of Misty in seconds.

'Will we make it?' he asked Chad.

'We've only got one chance, and that's for sure,' grunted the bosun.

A fast moving swell sweeping over the reef in a welter of foam thrust Misty forward. The sailors gritted their teeth, dreading a sudden lurch and the sound of splintering wood as the jagged coral slid close by, then cheered with relief as they drifted into the turquoise water of the lagoon to ground gently on the sand.

Ancell followed the crew ashore, paddling through clear water, a myriad of fish about his feet. He climbed the sand dunes and surveyed the parched landscape of dry grass and stunted shrub with foreboding. Nothing moved in the stifling heat, and he wondered if he had sailed half way round the world to die on such a desolate and unforgiving shore. Yet he knew this was the place he was meant to be. He was being called into that wilderness.

Protected from the blazing sun by Misty's foresail rigged as an awning, the sailors devoured the reef fish The Cook had netted and grilled over a fire of driftwood. Between mouthfuls they examined their predicament. There remained but two days' ration of rainwater saved during the passage, and they faced the grim prospect of dying of thirst.

'Look!' shouted Jobey, jumping up and pointing to the dunes. Everyone turned - and saw nothing.

'A boy! I saw a boy!' called Jobey, slipping and sliding as he struggled up the soft sand. He looked about wildly; then tramped back and flopped down.

'Sorry! I thought I saw someone,' he muttered.

'Don't worry about it! I've just seen a tankard of beautiful ale!' replied Chad.

'You can use your imagination now,' said The Cook, as he ladled out the last half mug of water for the day, tipping a little of his own into Merrie's. They sipped in silence, savouring every last drop. Chad rose, stretched, and suddenly stood stock-still.

'Bless you Jobey, you were right!' he whispered.

A boy was watching them from the foot of the dunes. Long legged and lithe, his sinewy body was as black as ebony. He held a wooden spear ready to throw.

'Who is he?' whispered Ancell to Doc. 'Do you know anything about these people?'

'He's an Aborigine. The name means "from the beginning". They've lived here for forty thousand years,' said Doc. 'You and I would soon die in these deserts, but they understand the plants and the creatures and know how to live off the land. He could be our salvation.'

Capt. Albern rose to his feet, but the boy held out a hand forbidding him to come closer.

'Do you come in peace?' he called.

'We do,' replied the captain.

'What brings you to my land?'

'We suffered damage in a storm and need to make repairs. But first we must find water or we will surely die.'

'Do you have guns?' asked the boy.

'We carry no arms and intend you no harm. All we ask is that you lead us to water.'

The boy lowered his spear and walked closer. 'My name is Jandamarra,' he said. 'I thought you might be like the men who cause such misery to my people.'

'What men?' asked Capt. Albern.

Misty's crew listened in silence as Jandamarra told of a ship that had landed on their shore a year ago. The crew had started to build a camp in the sacred valley where the spirits of his ancestors lived. The village elders walked a day to explain their forefathers could not rest in peace while they trespassed there. But even as they begged them to leave, the men had raised their guns and fired. His father had been hit in the shoulder.

'And they stay there still?' asked the captain.

'The ship sailed away, and we hoped they had gone,' said Jandamarra. 'But some men remained to build more huts, and now the ship has returned. It's anchored a little further up the coast.'

'You should drive them off,' said Skeet. 'I'll join you – we'll all join you. Guns or not, we'll soon send them running.'

Jandamarra shook his head. 'We would never fight on such holy ground.'

Ancell was thinking only of the voice that called him. He turned to Jandamarra.

'There is someone close by here I have to find, but I don't know who or where,' he blurted.

'He has dreams,' said Chad, shaking his head sadly.

Jandamarra stared at Ancell. 'The seer foretold someone would come,' he murmured. 'You must come with me. He will know if you are the one.'

Doc pricked up his ears. 'Is he a bone man, a sorcerer who projects the power of the death bones into his victims and turns them into rock?'

'He is not what you call a sorcerer,' replied Jandamarra sharply. 'We have doctors who protect us by speaking to the spirits, just as we have those who know which plants will heal the sick. It is something you would not understand.'

'I'd like to meet him,' persisted Doc.

'He will speak only to the dreamer,' said Jandamarra. 'Come!' he called to Ancell, and walked away. 'I will bring you food and water tomorrow,' he called over his shoulder.

'Now you've upset him,' Pickle admonished the owl. 'It would serve you right if the bone man changes you into a sparrow.'

'Or even better has you stuffed,' said Chips. 'Seeing as you're no use as a doctor we could make Misty a figurehead of you.'

'More likely he'll turn us all into stone,' grumbled Jobey.

Long shadows lay across the dunes as Ancell followed Jandamarra into the desert.

'Are we going to your village?' he asked.

'We will walk and he will find us.'

'Doc didn't mean to be rude. He reads lots of books and is very knowledgeable about things.'

'Books? Knowledge?' said Jandamarra. 'If he lived in our land a thousand years he might begin to learn.'

They walked on in silence, Ancell struggling to keep up even though the boy's pace appeared unhurried. The beach was long lost to view and the sky already dark to the east when Jandamarra halted. Ancell looked about him.

The desert spread unchanging in every direction, silent and mysterious, waiting for the cool of the night.

'It's a strange and beautiful place,' he said.

'And before the men came was more beautiful still,' said the Aborigine. 'You may go to him now.'

'Go where? There's no one here.'

Jandamarra pointed to an old man waiting motionless a few yards away, as if he had been there all the time. His hair was as white as Jandamarra's was black. He leaned on a staff, and looked too frail to walk, yet his eyes were as clear as Capt. Albern's. Unsure of the correct etiquette, Ancell made a deep bow. He was relieved there was not a bone in sight.

The seer did not speak, but beckoned him to sit. Ancell felt compelled to look up into the old man's eyes. Suddenly he began to see his dreams, but more vividly. He could see delicate tracings of silver on the pistol pointed at him. The image faded and for the first time he saw a beautiful star hanging low on the horizon. He could hear the seer speaking, but could not gather his thoughts to make sense of what he said. He felt himself falling and everything went dark. Then he saw the old man smiling down on him.

'We have waited a long time,' said the seer, 'but at last you have come.'

Ancell started to rise, but the seer lightly touched his shoulder with a wrinkled hand, laying such a weight on him he was unable to move. The old man talked quietly with Jandamarra, then raising his staff to Ancell in farewell, turned away.

'He says you may walk now,' called Jandamarra. He looked excited.

Ancell stumbled to his feet. He felt light headed and a little giddy, but full of energy. He watched the old man walk into the wilderness.

'Shouldn't we see him safely to his home?' he asked.

'He'll have walked twice the distance before I get you back,' said Jandamarra.

'He was reading my dreams, and I saw some more – but I don't understand what they mean or what he was telling me.'

'We can't see the future as he can.'

'He said he had been waiting for me.'

'And better still, I am to help you.'

'I don't see how.'

'You will tomorrow.'

'Why was I unable to stand?'

Jandamarra smiled. 'Maybe so you could tell your Doc you were turned to rock. Now save your breath for walking.'

CHAPTER 10

'That was good!' announced Pickle, with a long belch of satisfaction.

'Nothing like a good chicken stew,' agreed Chips.

'Lizard,' corrected The Cook.

'I suppose that's why I got the tail,' complained Jobey.

'Of course you did! Lizard is mostly tail,' said Waff.

'The very tip of it then,' Jobey persisted.

The crew sat beneath the awning waiting to hear what Ancell had to report. At first light, Jandamarra and two friends had delivered fresh water and a variety of foods, many of which were subtly flavoured roots and berries. Strangely they felt neither bloated nor sleepy however much they gorged themselves. Waff puffed on his pipe and squinted up at the cloudless sky.

'Any sign of rain?' he asked Doc.

Doc had salvaged a battered black umbrella from his belongings, which he had eventually managed to open and parade to the amusement of the Aborigines, who in turn had received a lecture on the dangers of sunstroke.

'It appears, like our hosts, you think a sensible precaution a source of amusement,' grumbled Doc. 'I'm surprised they found a parasol so hilarious; I'd have thought they'd have seen one before.'

'They probably have. It's you that's new to them. I expect they laughed all the way home,' explained Waff.

'We can't sit here all day. I'm going to get Ancell,' said Skeet, standing up impatiently.

'I tried to wake him to tell me about the bone man, but he was all curled up, so I couldn't,' said Merrie.

'Probably occupied with a dream,' said Chad, picking his teeth.

Ancell hurried across the beach. 'I've only just woken. Is there any food…'

'Was the bone man very frightening? Did he do magic?' interrupted Merrie.

'You look much the same so I suppose he didn't turn you to stone,' observed Doc.

'Did you ask him to extinguish Waff's pipe forever, as I requested?' asked Chips.

'He did nearly turn me into a rock,' Ancell informed Doc with a hint of superiority.

Everyone laughed.

'A plump, round one,' said Waff.

'But not as plump as he was,' said Thom.

'Not as fat,' confirmed Tam.

Ancell maintained a dignified silence. He was not receiving the rapt attention he deserved.

'So what happened?' asked Chad.

'We walked far into the desert,' Ancell commenced.

'Get to the point,' interrupted Skeet. 'What did you learn?'

Ancell paused dramatically.

'You won't believe this, but he saw my dreams!'

'So?' said everyone.

'You've been going on about them for so long, it's a mercy we all don't,' said Doc.

'Will you please just tell us what he told you,' Skeet pleaded.

'He told Jandamarra he was to help me.'

'He's helping us already. Did he tell you where to find whoever you are looking for?'

Ancell shifted uneasily. 'Not in so many words, but he did tell me things I don't understand, and I saw some more dreams.'

Chad's tail flicked with exasperation.

'More dreams! You wander off to meet your bone man friend…'

'Don't call him that! He's a wise man!' flashed Ancell.

'Wise man then – who you say you can't make sense of. Then you tell us you've got another dream. That's a great help!'

The rat rose to his feet and regarded the hedgehog sadly. 'There's one thing that really disappoints me though.'

'Which is?'

Chad smirked. 'You forgot to ask him for a tail!' he said, and skipped down the beach convulsed with laughter.

'You be careful yours doesn't fall off! You don't know what I asked him!' shouted Ancell.

Capt. Albern watched and smiled.

'Jandamarra's back,' announced Skeet, waving to the Aborigine.

Jandamarra was standing on the beach beckoning towards the dunes. A shock of tousled red hair appeared above a ridge. Jandamarra beckoned again and a freckle- faced girl ran down to clasp his hand. She regarded the crew half defiantly, half ready to run.

'Are you truly not pirates?' she called.

Captain Albern frowned. 'Certainly not!'

'Do we look like pirates?' protested Jobey. He pointed at Doc. 'Does he look like a cutthroat plunderer?'

The girl glanced at Doc and stifled a giggle.

'Come and sit in the shade,' invited Capt. Albern.

While the crew brushed the sand from the tarpaulin and made room for her, Jandamarra spoke quietly to Capt. Albern, then rested easily on his heels beside the girl.

'This is Sassy,' he said. 'I didn't tell you about her until the seer said she would be safe with you.'

'Jandamarra saved my life,' said Sassy. 'He found me dying of thirst in the desert and carried me to his village.'

'You may rest easy with us,' said Capt. Albern, and introduced the crew. Chips politely raised his bowler; everyone murmured their greetings, and then subjected the girl to a barrage of questions.

Capt. Albern called for silence. 'Please tell us your story,' he said.

'From the beginning?'

'From the very beginning.'

Sassy looked round the circle of faces and began her tale. She had been a laundress, working for Mrs Flood, a large bullying woman with beady eyes, who was always threatening her and the other girls she would put them on the street if they didn't scrub harder. From early morning to late at night they washed the clothes of sailors coming ashore, for which they received a mattress to sleep on and two bowls of soup a day.

One evening when she had at last been allowed to rest, Mrs Flood had called her. She had expected to be ordered to do yet another wash, but Mrs Flood had been all smiles and presented her to a lady as her best worker. The lady, who wore a beautiful scarlet dress and held a silk fan close to her face, had asked her where her parents were.

Sassy paused, struggling not to cry.

'Go on,' said Capt. Albern gently.

'I haven't got any.'

'Just like me!' interrupted Merrie.

Sassy glanced at him gratefully. 'You're very small,' she observed.

Merrie puffed out his chest. 'Yes, but I'm a sailor,' he replied.

'And then?' prompted Capt. Albern.

'The lady gave Mrs Flood some money and said I was to work for her in her mansion where I would be well looked after. I didn't want to go because the younger girls would have no one to comfort them when Mrs Flood made them cry, but Mrs Flood pushed me into the lady's carriage where two men gagged and blindfolded me. They rowed me to a ship and locked me in a cabin with Chantal and Max, who they'd kidnapped too. Chantal has a lovely voice. She sang in the streets and lived on the few coins people who stopped by to listen gave her. Max had made a home under an abandoned rowing boat on the beach. He collected driftwood to sell for kindling. They're orphans too. You see there is no one to remember us, no one to miss us.'

'Do you know the name of this ship?' asked Capt. Albern.

'It's called "The Executioner". The crew say it's because they show no mercy. The captain is a great brute of a man with a black beard.'

'Who is at his most dangerous when he laughs?'

Sassy nodded. 'He always laughs when he hangs someone. He laughs even more when he makes them walk the plank.'

Capt. Albern looked grim but said nothing.

'Laughing Jack – the most feared pirate ever to sail the high seas,' said Chad. 'Certain death is the fate of the unfortunate mariner who spies "The Executioner" on the horizon. They say he has sent innocent fishermen to the bottom for no more than the day's catch. He is believed to hide out in different parts of the world where he stashes his booty.'

'And now he defiles our land,' said Jandamarra.

'The woman is his Second in Command,' continued Chad. 'A Countess, it is told, who always dressed in white and was once the most talented and beautiful woman in Europe. She was found guilty of poisoning the aged Count for his fortune. The night before she was to be hanged, she lured a gaoler into her cell and cut him down with his own sword. They say she killed four men making her escape, although wounded herself. The blood stained her dress, since when she has worn only red.'

'The lady who kidnapped me,' confirmed Sassy. 'Scarletta is her name.'

'I would never have believed anyone would stoop as low as kidnapping children,' muttered Pickle.

'They say we're not the first and won't be the last.'

'Worked the others to death I expect,' said Jobey.

'How did you come to be here?' asked Capt Albern.

'The ship sailed and for many weeks we were made to scrub the decks and mend the sails. After we landed here, Laughing Jack sailed again and we only had to cook and clean for the crew building the camp. But not long ago he returned and made us work twice as hard. Chantal suffers the most because he makes her sing for him far into the night as well. She said he laughed when she fainted from exhaustion. That's when I decided to risk the desert in the hope of finding help.'

'How did you escape?' asked Skeet.

'One night they were all so drunk they forgot to lock my cell. The guard on the gate was asleep, so I fled.'

Ancell's heart was thumping. 'Sassy,' he asked, 'is anyone other than the three of you imprisoned there?'

Sassy shook her head. 'Not that I know of,

though when Laughing Jack returned I thought I once heard someone crying in the night.'

'Skipper, I've something to say,' announced Ancell. He rose to his feet and cleared his throat. 'Capt. Albern, Sassy, Jandamarra, fellow members of the crew and Doc,' he commenced.

'Spare us a speech,' groaned Jobey.

'Am I not a member of the crew?' protested Doc.

'If you've got something to say, get on with it,' grunted Chad.

Ancell tried again. 'I have already caused you much suffering to bring me this far. Though I don't know who calls me, at the very least my task is to free Chantal and Max. Now I must put you in danger no longer and go on alone.'

Capt. Albern and Jandamarra exchanged a smile.

'Don't be daft!' growled Chad. 'What are you going to do? Knock on Laughing Jack's door and say – "excuse me kind Sir, but I'm a dreaming hedgehog come to release your prisoners if you'd be so good!" You stick with your voices and leave the fighting to me.'

'We need to define our aims, shape a strategy, and decide our tactics,' announced Doc.

'You do your strategising and tacticking and I'll do something about it,' retorted Chad.

Capt. Albern called for silence. 'Jandamarra has already prepared a plan,' he said. 'He knows this land and we don't, so we will do as he says.'

'I will lead a rescue party to the camp,' said Jandamarra. 'The seer has forbidden me to go further, but I will wait for you.'

'But first we must make Misty seaworthy,' said Capt. Albern. 'Laughing Jack could discover us at any moment, and if we free Chantal and Max we will need to sail quickly. Until then, Sassy will be safer with the Aborigines.'

'What if the rescue party gets caught?' said Jobey.

'We trust Jandamarra will be able to help them escape. If they don't return by the morning of the third day we will know they're in trouble. It will be too dangerous to remain here, so we will sail, taking Sassy with us.'

There was a murmur of dismay. The captain unrolled a chart and pointed.

'Sail a day or so down the coast to this creek. The shore changes to forest, and Jandamarra says Misty will be well hidden. If the rescue party can escape, he will lead them to us.'

Larren pushed Merrie aside to study the chart more closely.

'Sounds good to me, Skipper,' said Skeet. 'Can I lead the search party? Anyone who tries to stop me will find my teeth at their throat!'

'I'm sorry,' answered the captain. His voice faltered. 'But without Truegard I need you on board.'

'Whoever goes will need to be fit,' said Jandamarra. 'You are not used to walking in my country and will find it hard.'

'That's us,' said Tam and Thom. Nobody argued.

'I can spare one of you,' said the captain. Tam and Thom drew straws.

'Tam's sailing,' said Thom.

'Thom's walking,' said Tam.

Larren listened. He decided accompanying the dreamy hedgehog might present an opportunity to turn events to his advantage.

'As a matter of fact I'm the strongest,' he stated, daring anyone to challenge him. He spoke directly to Ancell. 'I will go with you. You will recall I offered you my assistance long ago.'

'I remember,' admitted Ancell.

'In which case I think Chad should complete the party,' said Capt. Albern.

'You bet I should,' said Chad, looking hard at the grey squirrel.

Ancell glanced from Larren to Chad. Although Larren would make a powerful ally, he was pleased Chad would be there, however little the bosun thought of him.

'Time to get to work,' announced Capt. Albern.

Everyone set to with a will, convinced the rescue would be successful. All hands heaved every one of Misty's sails ashore until they stretched far down the beach for Waff to inspect.

Chips eased his aching back. 'Be nice to have some kids on board,' he observed.

'Our bosun will have to watch his language,' said Pickle, with a sidelong glance at Chad.

'Quite right!' agreed Jobey. 'I shall expect to hear, "please Mr Jobey, I should appreciate your assistance with this sail" and "thank you Mr Jobey for all your efforts" in future.'

Lost for a suitable retort, Chad could only scowl and stalk off.

For six days the sailors laboured from dawn to dusk. Misty was hauled first on one side and then the other to replace the damaged planking of her hull. The spars and rigging were repaired, the sails patched, and Merrie commenced a regimen of exercises, which he gasped to The Cook in the middle of his third and final press-up, would make him as fit as Jandamarra.

Denied the opportunity of meeting a bone man, refused a visit to the Aborigines' village, and forbidden to venture out of sight lest he got lost, Doc wandered the beach, detailed to collect driftwood for The Cook's fire. However he mainly returned with a collection of seashells, which he enthusiastically laid before an unimpressed cook and crew.

Ancell helped out wherever instructed, which was usually cleaning below decks. He was mopping out the fo'c'sle when Larren found him. The grey squirrel leaned at the door, watching.

'I'd have that miserable cook do a menial task like that,' he said.

'I'm neither a carpenter nor a sailmaker, and come to that I can't cook. This I can do,' snapped Ancell.

'On Chad's instructions I suppose. Not much of a job for a leader of an expedition.'

Ancell mopped all the harder.

'I wanted to speak to you about the rescue party,' continued Larren.

'What of it?'

'Young Thom is fit and you're in good condition, but that mangey rat worries me. He's obviously lost so many fights I wonder he can walk at all, let alone make a trek. I think he'd slow us down, and I wondered if you'd have a word with the captain about dropping him.'

Ancell leaned on the mop. 'So why don't you speak to the skipper?'

'Because you are the leader of the party,' replied Larren smoothly.

'In that case, I want Chad with me.'

Larren hesitated to say something more, then shrugged and left.

CHAPTER 11

Misty was floated a safe distance from the shore at high tide on the seventh day, patched but proud once more, and that night her crew slept soundly.

Ancell tossed and turned, worrying whether he would be able to keep up on the following day's trek and whether his resolve to free the children would hold. He worried too, whether he would lead them all to a sorry end.

Jandamarra was already waiting when the sailors rowed ashore at dawn. Capt. Albern drew Ancell aside.

'We have paid dearly to bring you this far,' he said. 'So follow your dream and do what you are called to do.'

Ancell looked into the sea otter's pale blue eyes, still clouded with sadness.

'I wish Truegard were here. He wouldn't fail you.'

'Think of Truegard at your side, and neither will you,' replied the captain.

The Cook wished them good luck, while vaguely looking around for Merrie, and an envious Skeet and Doc wished them well. Tam and Thom embraced silently.

'No heroics!' Capt. Albern instructed Chad. 'I'll be in trouble if I don't return you to Miss Strait in one piece.'

'You bet you will; I owe her three months rent,' said Chad.

Pickle, Jobey, Waff and Chips waved good-bye, Chips doffing his bowler for the occasion.

Jandamarra walked steadily, picking a path through the scrub without pause. Larren, Thom and Ancell followed in single file. Chad plodded after Ancell, insisting he would not have Larren at his back, and Jandamarra's two friends carrying food and water brought up the rear. The mid-morning sun beat down before Jandamarra allowed a halt. Ancell, Thom and Chad slumped to the ground, quenching their thirst. Larren stood apart, drinking deeply. The Aborigines took a few sips of water and waited to move on. Ancell was wondering if he dared ask how much further they had to go, when Jandamarra motioned everyone to keep quiet. The Aborigines listened and beckoned the sailors behind an outcrop of rock.

'We're being followed,' whispered Jandamarra, adding sombrely that the sailors left many tracks. Ancell could hear nothing but the thumping of his heart; it was beating so loud he was sure it would give them away.

Then Jandamarra sighed with exasperation as Merrie staggered into view. The harvest mouse took a few more steps and collapsed into semi-consciousness. Jandamarra's friends laid him on a litter fashioned from branches and grasses and Jandamarra held a flask of water to his lips.

'It's too late to take him back; we'll carry him,' he told Ancell.

The sun burned harder and Ancell began to tire. Head bent, sweat stinging his eyes and covered in the red dust kicked up when he stumbled, he concentrated on keeping up with the blurred figure of Thom ahead. If he looked around he saw only the same scorched wilderness unfolding in every direction, and he wondered how the Aborigines knew where they were going. Just as he thought he could go on no longer, Jandamarra waited by an island of rock and pointed to an opening.

'We'll rest here until nightfall,' he said.

The dim light of the cave was a respite from the glare of the desert. Ancell glanced about as the Aborigines laid out the food. Merrie slumbered on his stretcher. Larren sat with closed eyes, but looked as strong as ever.

'How do you feel?' he asked Thom.

Thom smiled. 'Fine – but next time Tam can do the walking,' she said.

'Give me a boat anytime,' grunted Chad. He nodded towards the Aborigines.

'Look at them! Not a speck of dust on them and as fresh as daisies. They certainly can walk.' Ancell handed the rat a flask of water. He thought he looked very tired.

The sailors slept deeply and the sun had long set before Ancell felt Jandamarra gently shake him awake. He rose stiffly, rubbing his aching muscles. The light of the waning moon threw the desert into stark relief, and he shivered in the chill of the night. He followed the shadow of Thom, beyond whom he could make out the dark figure of Larren, but of Jandamarra he could see nothing.

The terrain became harder and their progress slowed as they climbed a series of steep ridges. Ancell heard Chad slip and fall. He waited, but the rat waved him to keep moving. He tramped on, the moon throwing his shadow before him. Suddenly he caught up with Thom and Larren, standing with Jandamarra a few yards below the top of a ridge. Jandamarra waited for Chad, then held a finger to his lips and beckoned them forward.

Creeping to the crest, Ancell looked down on two rough-hewn wooden buildings connected by a short passageway. His heart jumped at how close they were. Lamplight filtered from the larger one, and through an open door he could see two men playing cards and taking turns to swig from a bottle. One had a spotted kerchief tied about his head and the other wore a black patch over one eye. Another doorway revealed what appeared to be an armoury. Parts of cannons lay about the floor and muskets lined the wall. Barrels of gunpowder were piled in an untidy heap close by. The smaller building lay in darkness, the bars on a line of small windows glinting in the moonlight. A wooden palisade enclosed the compound where packhorses and mules were stabled in a corner beside a pair of long sturdy canoes. Two armed men lounged at the gate.

Jandamarra pointed to the canoes. 'They're our fishing boats,' he whispered. 'They stole them from the beach.'

'Those barred windows look like cells,' said Chad. 'I reckon we should look there first.'

Thom pointed. 'We could try that door in the passageway. If we climb in at the opposite end to the gate we'll be out of sight of the guards.'

Ancell was staring at the height of the fence.

'What if the door is bolted?' he said.

'We'll try the windows.'

'We couldn't get through those bars.'

Merrie squeezed between them, refreshed and excited.

'I could,' he said.

'I'll go down and have a closer look, then we'll have a think what to do,' said Ancell.

'That won't get us anywhere. We have to get in and think as we go along,' said Chad.

'Are you sure you can climb through those bars?' Thom asked Merrie.

'Easy!' said Merrie, his eyes sparkling.

'Then let's go!' said Chad.

'We'll wait for you until tomorrow night,' whispered Jandamarra. 'If you're caught I've a plan for your escape.' He pointed to where the ridge rose to a rocky crag. 'If you see fire all around you, do not be afraid, but flee in that direction. Put your trust in us and you will come to no harm. Now go; you have three hours before dawn.'

Ancell followed Chad over the ridge, too agitated to ask Jandamarra what he meant. Once, the rat dislodged a stone, and they froze as it tumbled down the hill, only breathing again when at last it rolled to a halt. Thom scaled the fence first, easing herself over and climbing down into the compound. Larren and Chad followed; then Merrie scampered over with easy agility. Ancell searched for a gap to crawl through.

'Come on!' breathed Chad. 'You can climb a fence can't you!'

Ancell glared at him through a crack in the stakes. 'Of course I can. It's just that I'm not sure about getting over the top.'

'Just climb. I'll catch you.'

Ancell climbed, rolled over the top, missed his footing, flattened Chad and winded himself.

He lay still, praying the guards would not come running. Thom beckoned and they made a dash for the cover of the buildings; then inched towards the door. There was no handle.

'It's bolted on the inside,' whispered Chad.

Thom pointed to a window and hoisted Merrie onto her shoulders. Merrie squeezed through the bars, dropped lightly to the floor, then jumped and pulled on the bolt. They held their breath as the door creaked open and one by one crept into the passageway. A murmur of voices came from their left. They turned right and sidled round a corner into a corridor of doors.

'These must be the cells,' whispered Thom, reaching for the key hanging above the first door.

Moonlight threw the pattern of the window bars onto the bare walls of the room and revealed a straw mattress on the dusty floor. A girl's clothes lay crumpled in a corner.

'These could be Sassy's,' whispered Ancell. 'Stay here while I try the other doors. If I'm caught you might stand a chance of getting away.'

'Seems sensible,' murmured Larren.

'We're coming with you,' said Chad. 'If we have to fight our way out we'll do it together.'

The second and third cells were bare and Ancell's hopes dwindled. Thom eased open the fourth door and beckoned. A sleeping girl lay beneath a torn blanket, her head cradled on one arm. Ancell gently shook her shoulder. She sat up with a start, one hand brushing long flaxen tresses from her face, the other holding the blanket protectively about her.

'Don't be afraid,' whispered Ancell quickly. 'We're friends of Sassy.'

Chantal's cornflower blue eyes clouded. 'Sassy died in the desert. The pirates told us. Who are you?'

'No she didn't, and we've come to get you and Max out.'

'Is Sassy truly alive?'

'She's safe with the Aborigines.'

Chantal clasped her hands together. 'That's wonderful! So wonderful!' she breathed. 'Can you really rescue us? Max is in the next cell.'

Thom slipped out of the door.

'Are there any other children apart from you and Max?' asked Ancell.

Chantal shook her head. 'Not that I know of.'

Thom led a stockily built, snub-nosed boy with sandy hair into the cell. Max ran to Chantal and flung his arms about her.

'Sassy did escape! And so will we!' he said, his eyes brimming with excitement.

'Let's go,' whispered Chad.

They crept along the corridor, Ancell in the

lead. He paused at the end and listened hard; then turned the corner into the passageway. A heavy hand grabbed his throat, pinning him to the wall. He heard Chantal scream and recognised the card player with the spotted kerchief.

'Got you! You scoundrel!' growled the man. 'Steal our dear sweet little workers would you?'

'I told you I heard that door squeak,' said the man with the eye patch from the doorway.

Chad stepped towards him.

'You ought to get those hinges fixed,' he said.

'Stand back!' ordered the man.

'I think it's the top one that's binding,' continued Chad, edging closer.

The man drew a pistol from his belt. 'Stay where you are or I'll ...'

Chad sprang, knocking the pistol aside as it fired. At the same moment Thom butted the man half throttling Ancell. The man gasped and lashed out at her, but Thom caught his fist and twisted his arm behind his back. Merrie rushed forward and bit him on the leg.

'Run! All of you!' shouted Chad, wrestling his man to the ground.

'Hurry! Take the children!' panted Thom, jerking the man's arm higher.

Ancell broke free, but as he grabbed Chantal and Max, two other men ran down the passageway to bar the door. Two others followed. One coshed Thom across the back of the neck and the other stooped to strike Chad's head with the butt of his pistol. The man with the eye patch staggered to his feet and aimed a kick at the stunned rat. He recovered his breath and kicked again. Larren watched.

A giant of a man with a black beard strode forward. He wore heavy sea boots and a wine stained nightshirt open to the waist, revealing a barrel chest of thick curly hair. A silver earring hung from one ear; the other was half cut away. Stroking his thick lips with a dirty finger, he lifted Chad's head with his foot, then letting it fall, scowled at Ancell. Beneath the heavy eyebrows, his small round eyes were as black as the night.

'You've disturbed my sleep,' growled Laughing Jack. He smiled. 'I'll hang you in the morning.'

Thrown in a cell, Ancell cursed himself for not moving faster when Chad and Thom had attacked. Thom clung to the window bars of her cell, rubbing her throbbing neck. She saw a shadowy figure in the compound, and for a wild moment thought it was Tam, but it was only a pirate inspecting the palisade. Merrie made several running jumps at his window, but it was too high for him to reach, so he set himself to scratching his name on the wall in the tradition of all heroic prisoners. Chad came to with a groan, and as a matter of routine stretched each limb in turn to test for broken bones. Swimming in and out of consciousness he struggled to remember what particular fight had laid him there. Then his mind cleared and he recalled the grey squirrel stepping away when he was most needed.

'If it's the last thing I do, I'll get you for that,' he growled.

Larren slowly paced his cell, plotting how to work their imprisonment to his advantage. He assumed they would be interrogated and began to rehearse what he would say.

On board Misty, The Cook wandered about the deck, unable to sleep. Too late he had found Merrie's scrawled note stating he had decided to become a trekker to free the children and would be back soon. Furious with himself for allowing the harvest mouse to slip away, and angry with Merrie for his foolhardiness, he prayed that he was safe with the search party. He watched Tam climb from the fo'c'sle.

'Can't you sleep either,' he said.

Tam stood at the rail, looking to the shore. 'I've got a splitting headache. Thom's been hurt,' he said.

CHAPTER 12

Ancell stood at the window of his cell, watching the shadow of the stockade shorten as the morning wore on. The pirates had twice amused themselves by offering him water, but after being ordered to kneel and beg for a sip, he had been pinned to the wall while a sniggering man held the flask to his face and dribbled the precious liquid to the floor. The sun was high before a key rattled in the lock a third time.

'I'm not thirsty,' he said, without turning. The two men said nothing, but propelled him along the corridor.

'The captain requests the pleasure of your company,' said one, pushing open a door.

'You can ask him for a nice long drink!' said the other, and they both laughed.

The sparsely furnished room was lit only by a shaft of light from a single heavily barred window. Laughing Jack stood in a corner, his massive hands cupped together. He opened his fingers and watched the shower of glittering jewels tumble into the iron-banded chest at his feet.

'Gold, silver and pearls,' he gloated. 'Diamonds, emeralds, sapphires and rubies – and all mine.' Wiping his lips he wheeled round. 'And you would dare to rob me of them!'

'I came for the children,' said Ancell.

'Don't fool with me! Who would bother about a few worthless children? It's my treasure you were after.'

The two men at the door jumped aside as a woman stepped into the room. She was dressed in red, even to the crimson ribbon that tied her long lustrous black hair. Her high cheekbones accentuated dark sultry eyes, and she moved with a cat-like grace. She was very beautiful. She turned and Ancell saw the scar. The jagged gash curved the length of her cheek to the corner of her delicate mouth, marring the soft olive skin with a sickle of white. Involuntarily he caught his breath.

'Yes! Look on it!' hissed Scarletta. 'I am marked for life, and whoever crosses my path will pay for it. What would you have with our children? Who sent you?'

'Nobody sent me. I was called in my dreams,' answered Ancell. 'How do you imagine I found you from half a world away.'

'He's mad,' grunted Laughing Jack, but Ancell thought he looked a little unnerved.

'Dreamers can be dangerous if they follow their dreams,' murmured Scarletta. She gazed at

Ancell. 'But sadly for you, your dreams are your downfall. The children will remain here as long as they live.'

'Were you fool enough to think they'd ever leave alive to tell the world where I am?' snarled Laughing Jack.

Ancell took a chance. 'Sassy will anyway if you don't release Chantal and Max,' he said quietly.

Laughing Jack stared at him open mouthed. A shadow of alarm crossed Scarletta's face. She recovered her composure quickly, but Ancell noticed the scar was flushed with red.

'The girl is dead,' she said.

'She's alive and well.'

Laughing Jack breathed hard, the veins at his temples throbbing. Snatching a knife from his belt he held the shaking blade hard against Ancell's chest.

'Give me the girl,' he rasped. 'Hand the girl to me or I'll cut your heart out.'

'I don't have her.'

'Then tell me where she is or I'll boil you in oil. I'll pull your spines out one by one and have you roasted. I'll throw you to my crew for target practice until you beg to die.'

Ancell struggled to stay calm. 'Do as you will,' he said. 'But Sassy is safe with the Aborigines where you'll never find her.'

Laughing Jack clenched the knife to strike. Ancell closed his eyes.

'Wait!' said Scarletta sharply.

Laughing Jack stepped back, and trembling with fury, hurled the knife. The blade quivered in the wall close above Ancell's head.

'You can play with him later,' said Scarletta. 'I think we should speak to the others first. No doubt we can persuade them to be a little more helpful. Lock him up,' she ordered the men at the door.

'If you don't give us water we'll soon all be dead anyway,' croaked Ancell, and collapsed.

He came to with a guard throwing a bucket of dirty water over his head. A flask of water and some stale bread had been placed in his cell. He drank deeply.

'Are the others getting any?' he asked.

The man grinned. 'Every one of them – I've told them to enjoy it as it will be their last,' he said, and slammed the door.

Merrie was devouring the last crumbs of his food when he was marched in front of Laughing Jack.

'Merrie Prentice, Able Seaman First Class,' he announced. He thought he should have a number. 'Number One,' he added.

Scarletta knelt and gently stroked his face.

'Relax, Merrie – I want to help you,' she soothed. 'Tell me where Sassy is and you and your friends can go free.'

Merrie flinched at the touch of her fingers.

'Able Seaman Prentice Number One,' he repeated.

'Get him out of here!' ordered Laughing Jack impatiently, and Merrie, head held high, was returned to his cell.

'If you'd let me work on him I could have talked him round,' sighed Scarletta.

'I haven't time to listen to baby harvest mice pretending to be prisoners of war,' snapped Laughing Jack.

Thom casually dismissed the array of jewels offered her for information, saying that none of them suited her. She then yawned at the promise of execution and explained that if Laughing Jack did not release them, her brother soon would.

The guards kept a firm hold on Chad, who in answer to Laughing Jack's furious questioning, replied that he had been strolling by, picking wild flowers, and had only broken in to see where the nasty smell was coming from. All Laughing Jack learned in no uncertain terms was what Chad thought of him.

Larren disdainfully broke the hold of the guards and faced Laughing Jack.

'About time!' he growled. 'I can offer you a deal.'

'I don't bargain with common thieves,' retorted Laughing Jack.

'Don't associate me with that rabble,' replied

Larren. 'I don't care what happens to the children. As you are aware I neither attacked your men nor sought to flee.'

Laughing Jack's eyes narrowed. 'Then why are you here?'

'Give me water and I'll tell you.'

Scarletta signalled a pirate to hand the grey squirrel a flask.

'You drink it,' Larren instructed.

Scarletta sipped. Larren snatched the flask and drank quickly.

'Haven't you touched the food and water brought to you?' asked Scarletta.

'It could have been drugged'

'You don't trust us, and we certainly don't trust you, so maybe we can do business,' reflected Scarletta.

Larren drank again and told of how, having escaped the mutineers, he had in effect become a prisoner on Misty, and likely to be blamed for the death of the first mate.

'And I'd guess rightly so,' murmured Scarletta.

'Shall we stop sparring,' snapped Larren. 'I assume you want the girl who escaped. I can help you. Give me what I want and I'll see Sassy is yours.'

'Nobody dictates to me,' bristled Laughing Jack. 'I can have you shot this moment.'

'But you won't because you want the girl.'

'And what do you want?' asked Scarletta.

'Their ship.'

'The girl for us and the ship for you,' mused Laughing Jack. 'I think we understand each other. Where are those Aborigines hiding her?'

'No one knows. But tomorrow they're putting her aboard the ship, which will hide in a creek. Give me sufficient well-armed men and you can take the girl and me the ship before they sail.'

Laughing Jack shook his head. 'Brainless as they are, those Aborigines are canny. As soon as they see us heading for the coast they'll disappear and the girl with them.'

'I told you to pretend to make friends with them,' said Scarletta.

'I should have shot them all in the first place,' grumbled Laughing Jack.

'Do you know where the creek is?' Scarletta asked Larren.

'I made sure I had a good look.'

Laughing Jack unrolled a chart.

Larren pointed. 'Just beyond this headland.'

'Perfect!' said Scarletta – 'we'll use the Aborigines' canoes to board the ship and recapture the girl.'

Laughing Jack began to laugh. 'And we can hang the ship's crew at the same time. I'm so excited I could hang someone right now!'

'Why not the rat who caused your men so

much trouble? I'm sure they'd like to see him swing,' said Larren.

'He can dig his grave tomorrow with the rest of them. Then we'll watch them all swing together,' said Laughing Jack.

Returned to his cell, where a meal and a carafe of wine were brought to him, Larren hurried to the window at the sound of hooves in the compound. The pirates were leading the mules from the stable and testing makeshift slings to carry the canoes.

He smiled. 'Thank you Ancell, you pathetic dreamer,' he murmured. 'Not only have you failed the children, but you have made me master of Misty. I win, you lose.'

Jandamarra, too, watched. He had long feared the rescue party had been captured, and now it seemed Laughing Jack was preparing to attack Misty. With a heavy heart, he instructed his companions to collect Sassy from the village and deliver her to Capt. Albern. Then, cursing the men who desecrated his forefathers' resting place, he walked fast in the direction of the ship.

CHAPTER 13

Tam pushed his untouched breakfast towards Chips, who, with his mouth full, nodded his thanks.

'You should eat - worrying won't help,' said Skeet. 'Maybe the children are slowing them down on the way back.'

Tam shook his head. 'Thom is in trouble. They've been caught. We'll be sailing without them,' he replied, and climbed to the crowsnest for the fourth time since first light to stare over the dunes. Suddenly, as if by magic, Jandamarra appeared on the beach. He was alone, and though prepared for disappointment, Tam's heart sank. By the time he and Pickle had rowed the gig ashore, Jandamarra's friends had emerged from the dunes with Sassy at their side. Sassy embraced the two Aborigines and stepped into the boat with Jandamarra, Sassy waving good-bye to her friends all the while she was ferried to Misty.

Captain and crew listened anxiously while Jandamarra told of how he had watched the search party break in successfully, but had seen no sign of them since. He was also concerned that Laughing Jack was preparing the canoes to attack Misty.

'Either that or he'll board "The Executioner" and blow us out of the water from the sea,' added Jobey.

Sassy turned to Capt. Albern. 'If you can't save Chantal and Max, I want to go back. I can't leave them by themselves. Anyway, once Laughing Jack's got me, maybe he'll let your crew go.'

'There's still a chance they might all escape,' replied the captain. 'Remember Jandamarra has a plan.'

'But we don't have the weapons to fight,' said Skeet.

'Fear is our weapon,' said Jandamarra. 'Something the pirates will fear enough to abandon the camp in a panic for long enough for both the children and your shipmates to flee.'

'I know!' interrupted Doc. 'Your seer will threaten them with the death bones!'

'Fire,' replied Jandamarra. 'We shall set fire to the land. The pirates will panic because they will think only of fighting it, which will be impossible. But we understand fire. We make it work for us. It burns where we wish, and it stops burning where we wish.'

The sailors shifted uneasily. Fire on board a ship usually meant death.

'I've read about this,' said Doc. 'You select an area of land and burn off all the dying vegetation to encourage new growth, which in turn attracts more wildlife. You can direct the fire at will. Can I come and help?'

'No!' answered Misty's crew in unison even before Jandamarra could shake his head, a response which Doc thought harsh, though predictable.

'I must leave, we must act tonight,' said Jandamarra, and shyly offered Capt. Albern an intricate carving. The spirit of the totem, he explained, would help protect Misty from evil. In turn, Capt. Albern presented the Aborigine with a scale model of Misty, delicately carved by Chips late into many a night. She sailed proudly on a sea of cotton wool in a bottle, and Waff, who had tied the rigging, carefully demonstrated how her masts were lowered to slide her through the neck.

Tam rowed Jandamarra ashore, accompanied by Capt. Albern as a matter of courtesy.

'One day I'll come back and see you,' shouted Sassy.

'And we will welcome you,' called back the Aborigine.

Capt. Albern took Jandamarra's hand. 'We may not meet again. Thank you, and please thank your people. With your help we shall yet prevail.'

'I pray you will. And perhaps one day the sacred resting place of our forefathers will be returned to them,' answered Jandamarra.

Misty's crew lined the rail to watch the lithe, angular, youth, who loved his land, bid farewell to the stoop backed otter, who belonged to the sea.

'Crocodylus porosus! I hope we see one,' exclaimed Doc suddenly.

'What are you on about now!' muttered Jobey.

'Estuarine crocodiles – the creek will be their habitat. Amazing creatures! They can live to be a hundred, and they can go for a year without food.'

'So if we throw Chips overboard the rest of us should be safe for several months,' suggested Waff.

'I don't know why Jandamarra didn't take you with him. You're good at setting fire to things,' retorted Chips. Waff grinned and luxuriated in lighting his first pipe of the day.

Tam and Capt. Albern heard the creak of the windlass and the rattle of chain as they stepped into the gig. Skeet was shortening the anchor.

Tam smiled. 'You'll lose your ship if we don't hurry,' he said. 'Mr Skeet is getting impatient.'

'And on this occasion rightly so – the sooner we hide Misty the better,' replied the captain.

Within minutes Misty pointed to the gap in the reef. Her crew gazed back at the beach shimmering in the heat, as lonely and deserted as when they had first stumbled ashore. Then they set more sail, their hearts filled with fresh hope, and turned south.

Merrie scratched another line on the wall of his cell to mark the second day of his incarceration. He thought being a prisoner was a lonely business, and wished that The Cook, if he were not too angry with him, would come to his rescue. Thom sat with her back to a wall, gazing at the light streaming through the window. She imagined herself beside Tam with the wind on her face as Misty sailed. Chad reflected on two failed attempts to escape, once by rolling on the floor feigning illness and hitting out at the guard who stooped over him, and once by a surprise attack from behind the door. But the guards worked in pairs, and all he could count for his efforts were some more bruises and the loss of two meals. Ancell shuffled round and round his cell for hour after hour. He tried to think of Truegard, who would never give up. But the red squirrel was dead, and he felt only despair.

Larren stood in the compound with Laughing Jack and Scarletta, watching the mules bearing the canoes file through the gate, followed by a train of packhorses laden with muskets and ammunition.

'We'll ride out after them later,' said Laughing Jack. He laughed. 'But first we have some hanging to do.'

Ancell blinked as a guard marched him into the compound. Even the late afternoon light hurt his eyes after the dimness of the cell. Pushed to where Chad, Thom and Merrie were standing, his heart leaped to see them unharmed. Then fear gripped at his throat as he saw the line of gallows. He had dreamed and hoped, but now he faced the reality of failure. He looked to the line of hills beyond the stockade, already tinted a deeper red by the last sunset he would see. Suddenly for the briefest of moments he saw the tall upright figure of Truegard waiting in the glow of the evening, and thrilled at a sudden unshakable assurance that they were not alone.

'We're going to be saved. I'm certain of it. Something will happen,' he whispered to Chad.

A grinning pirate threw shovels at their feet and ordered them to dig.

'You want holes, you dig them,' Ancell told him.

The man drew a pistol and snapped back the firing pin.

'What are we digging for - water, gold, potatoes?' asked Chad quickly.

'It makes a difference how you go about it,' added Thom.

The man lowered the gun. 'Just dig a hole big enough to lie in, and get moving,' he ordered. Slowly they started to dig.

Chad paused and leaned on his shovel.

'Where's the grey squirrel, or has he escaped you already?' he asked a guard.

The man pointed to the gallows. Larren was adjusting the length of the nooses.

'Traitor!' yelled Chad. Larren turned and sauntered towards them, stopping a safe distance off.

'Bye bye,' he said.

Bitter tears pricked Ancell's eyes. 'Why?' he demanded. 'You said you'd help us. We saved your life. Why turn against us?'

The grey squirrel shrugged. 'Because it is in my interest to do so.'

'You make me sick,' growled Chad. 'If you'd fought with us we were in with a chance. What's wrong with you – scared of getting your fur ruffled? You're a yellow-livered treacherous coward.'

'And you're nothing but a Common rat, and common you certainly are. The more of your kind that dig their own graves the better,' sneered Larren.

'I'd like to dig yours, I'd dig it very deep,' fumed Chad. 'And I'll tell you what else I'd like to do ...'

He stopped speaking and wrinkled his nose. Thom sniffed the air – then Ancell caught the faintest smell of burning. Merrie saw the first fire, a small patch of flickering flame and a wisp of smoke to the south. Thom pointed to another to the north. As the sun dipped below the ridge, casting the valley into shadow, they stood awestruck as another and yet another flared into life. Ancell thought he glimpsed the shadowy figures of the Aborigines flitting through the twilight, beating the fires towards the compound, and as he watched, each blaze ran to join another until they were encircled by a ring of flame. But for the dirt track that ran from the gate, the desert was alight.

Laughing Jack and Scarletta hurried into the compound and Larren ran to join them. The guards nervously fingered the triggers of their guns. 'Don't try anything or we shoot,' warned one.

Ancell noticed Chad eying up the distance to spring. 'Wait!' he whispered. 'They'll soon run of their own accord.'

'Maybe,' agreed Chad. 'It's that grey squirrel I'd like to get hold of. I knew there was something nasty about him.'

Ancell remembered how impressed he had been by Larren, and how he had considered him superior to Chad, and felt ashamed.

Laughing Jack cursed as his lieutenants

reported that the ring of fire was mysteriously closing in from every direction, and the men sent to beat it out had been driven back by the heat. He stared about wildly. All around flames were leaping into the night. Men ran from the buildings in a panic. Others jostled at the gate where the guard crazily fired his musket in the air. Scarletta rode through the confusion, leading a string of frightened horses with the ease of an accomplished horsewoman. A fight broke out at the gate.

'Come back, you fools!' roared Laughing Jack. 'We're on bare earth. The camp won't burn.' Then he swore as the gate swung open and the men disappeared down the track, shouting and cursing as they ran, until all he could hear was the crackle of the invading flames.

'We must get the horses out,' urged Scarletta. 'Whether the camp burns or not, we still want Sassy. What do we do with the other children and those interfering animals?'

Laughing Jack heaved his weight onto a horse. 'No time to bother about them,' he snapped. 'Even if they escape, the track is the only way out. I'll make sure they don't get far. You're riding with me. I'm not letting you out of my sight,' he ordered Larren.

Larren took the reins of a horse and mounted. Laughing Jack dug in his heels and fled at a gallop. Larren's horse raced after it, whether he liked it or not. Smoke drifted into the compound and the nostrils of Scarletta's horse flared. It reared, pawing the air, its ears flattened with fear. Little by little she pacified the terrified animal, and leading the two other horses, trotted for the gate.

'Looks like you're being deserted,' Ancell informed the guards. The men glanced at the departing riders and ran.

'Quick! Get the children!' said Chad.

They sprinted into the building and along the empty corridor. Thom reached for the keys to Chantal and Max's cells and threw open the doors.

'We're going to be free!' sang Chantal.

'I knew you would come!' said Max.

'The track isn't burning, we'll have to take our chance along it,' said Chad.

'Which is exactly where Laughing Jack will be,' said Thom.

'We'll do as Jandamarra instructed and walk towards the crag on the ridge,' said Ancell.

'But that's straight into the fire!' argued Chad.

'That's what he told us to do, and we must trust him. Let's go!' said Ancell.

They raced across the compound, lit a glowing red. Chantal and Max punched the air as they dashed through the gate. The fire was already skirting the camp. Ancell led the way, edging close to the stockade. It seemed madness to step into the blazing desert, but as he looked to the peak of the ridge, a narrow path opened between the flames, and in the distance he saw the figure of an Aborigine.

'That's Jandamarra, who saved Sassy,' he told Chantal and Max. 'Trust him.'

Thom took a deep breath, told Chantal, Max and Merrie to stay close behind, and began to climb.

Chad contemplated the licking flames. 'After you,' he muttered to Ancell.

Breathing harshly, Ancell stumbled towards the ridge, drifting smoke stinging his eyes. He was not far below Jandamarra when he slowed and stopped. A voice was calling him urgently. Someone was still imprisoned in the compound.

Wheezing and coughing, Chad caught up.

'Keep going! This is no place for a daydream. My whiskers are getting singed,' he gasped.

'I have to go back. We've left someone behind.'

'Don't be stupid! We've got the children. Be practical for once.'

'I have to. I know there's someone there.'

'Then I'll come with you.'

Ancell gripped the rat. 'You must go on. For Chantal and Max's sake you must get them safely aboard Misty before daybreak. That's being practical.'

'I suppose you're right,' admitted Chad, 'but I don't like it. For goodness sake keep your wits about you. Being a dreamer doesn't stop you getting roasted.'

Ancell plunged down the hill, cursing himself for not conducting a proper search. Once, he missed the edge of the path and yelped as he kicked up a shower of flickering sparks that drifted before him on the night breeze. Exhausted by the heat, the effort of the climb and his headlong dash, he tripped as he scuttled through the gate. A sharp stab of pain shot up his left leg – then he heard the thudding of hooves and looked up at Laughing Jack.

Laughing Jack slowly dismounted. 'Don't bother to get up,' he snarled, and drawing a pistol from his belt began to laugh. Ancell recognised the silver engraving on the gun. He lay still, his heart racing as he watched Laughing Jack's finger tighten on the trigger. Unable to think of anything to say to buy even a few seconds, he curled and waited for the end. A blinding flash of flame seared his eyes. He heard the whoof of an explosion and a blast of heat rolled him over. Slowly, to his amazement, he realised that he was still alive. He uncurled to see Laughing Jack crawl to his feet and stumble towards the gate after his fleeing horse. Another keg of gunpowder exploded, licking the armoury wall with flame, and black acrid smoke enveloped the compound. Half stunned and gritting his teeth, Ancell hobbled for the passageway door. There was another explosion and he could feel the heat as the fire took hold of the buildings. Smoke billowed down the corridor. He heard a wall collapse and knew he had only minutes before he was engulfed in flame. Every cell was empty. Beginning to panic, he checked Sassy's cell again, gasping for breath as he leaned against a wall to take the weight from his aching leg. That there was someone to be found he was certain, but though he tried to stay calm and think, an overwhelming desire to run numbed his mind.

'Help me!' he pleaded and slumped hopelessly to the floor. Then he heard the sound of distant sobbing.

A narrow corridor he had not noticed before led to a single door. With a final effort he jumped for the key to the lock. A weeping boy lay huddled in the corner of the cell. A larger explosion shook the building and the boy curled tighter, barely breathing.

'It's all right! I'm here,' shouted Ancell above the crash of a falling roof.

Slowly the boy uncurled. White faced, hollow cheeked and pitifully thin, he stared up with large brown eyes wet with tears, and briefly smiled.

'You've come,' he whispered.

Ancell knelt beside him. It was the voice that had called him for so long.

'What's your name?' Ancell asked.

'No name,' the boy whispered.

Ancell dragged him to his feet as flames licked at the doorway.

'Time to get out of here, Noname,' he urged. 'Can you walk?'

Trembling, Noname brushed a shock of dark hair from his forehead and nodded.

Seared by the heat, the smoke catching at their throats and barely able to see, they stumbled along the corridor to burst from the building. They turned, coughing and spluttering as the flaming timbers of the passageway crashed to the ground close behind them. Ancell pointed to the gate, barely visible through the billowing smoke, and gulping for breath, they picked their way through the burning debris of the camp.

Leading the fleeing party to the top of the ridge, Jandamarra span round at the crump of the exploding gunpowder to see pillars of flame leaping into the night. Chad stared in horror, wishing he had argued harder with the hedgehog, although he knew in his heart there was no stopping Ancell going back.

'Perhaps he's out and on his way,' said Thom, but she didn't sound convinced.

'He's got to be!' pleaded Merrie.

'He knows what he's doing,' said Chad gruffly, and wished he believed it.

Jandamarra stared at the burning buildings. He had not counted on carelessly stored gunpowder, nor had he envisaged the incineration of the compound. But now he watched with quiet joy as the flames seared the land clean of the evil the intruders had laid upon it. Now his ancestors' spirits would be able to return to live in peace, and he prayed the deliverance of that sacred place had not cost the hedgehog his life. He took a final look at the inferno and turned away.

'We must hurry if we're to reach cover by daybreak,' he said. 'Walk steadily and stay together.'

One by one they slipped and slithered down the steep slope towards safety somewhere ahead in the darkness. Chad followed last, often stopping to listen and peer back for a sign of his dreaming, wilful friend.

CHAPTER 14

A following breeze helped Misty make good progress as she followed the coast southward. Even so, evening was drawing in before the parched shoreline gave way to increasing scrub and eventually dense forest.

'Nice to see a bit of green,' said Chips, lounging by the rail.

Waff contemplated the tangled mass of jungle hanging over the water.

'We'll have to stand off until morning. No chance of finding a creek in that lot in the dark,' he observed.

'All hands aft!' called Skeet.

'Everyone on deck tonight,' Capt. Albern announced. 'If the search party break out we need to take them on board and sail immediately - so we'll risk going into the creek at high tide tonight. We've got one chance of making it without going aground, so keep alert and act fast. Any questions?'

'When will we reach the creek?' asked Tam.

'About three in the morning. The Cook is preparing dinner now, so you've time to eat and rest before we go close in.'

The crew headed for the galley thoughtfully. Sailing Misty close to an unknown shore in pitch dark and turning into an inlet they would not be able to see would require the finest navigation.

'That's not much to see me through to breakfast,' grumbled Jobey, staring at his plate.

'The skipper's ordered another meal for you once we're safely at anchor,' said The Cook with a sigh.

'Two dinners in one night?'

'You'll have earned it,' said Skeet. 'Remember, one mistake and we'll be aground for twelve hours.'

'Assuming we don't sink,' muttered Jobey.

'The skipper will do it easy,' said Chips. 'I remember him taking her through a harbour entrance so narrow you could step off on either side, not that you could see it in the fog. Howling gale it was too – I could feel the spray from the rocks as I stood at the helm.'

'Really?' said Sassy.

'Not really,' said Waff. 'There was a bit of a sea mist and a heavy swell. As for Chips on the helm, he couldn't sail a toy duck across a bath.'

'I was referring to an occasion you were not present,' huffed Chips.

'How do we find an entrance we can't see?' queried Doc.

'We follow the sea bed,' explained Skeet. 'The skipper will take us inshore until it shallows to five fathoms; then he'll track that line on the chart along the coast until the water deepens at the creek.'

'But how do we know how deep the water is?'

'Tam will take soundings with the lead line.'

'I could do that!' objected Jobey, 'Tam's the best on the helm.'

'You'd drop it, then where would we be,' said Pickle.

'So who will take the wheel?' persisted Jobey.

'You will,' Skeet informed him. 'Pickle, Chips and Waff are to man the yards.'

'Great!' muttered Jobey, 'I suppose when we end up half way up a tree in the jungle it'll all be my fault.'

'Correct!' confirmed his shipmates.

'Where is my assistance required?' demanded Doc.

Skeet suspected Misty was more likely to operate smoothly if the owl retired to his cabin.

'Your night vision is good. You can stand at the bow as a lookout,' he suggested.

'Aye aye Sir,' responded Doc smartly, and started to scramble for'ard.

'Not now Doc! I'll tell you when,' said Skeet with a sigh.

'And not before we put a line round you before you fall overboard,' added Pickle.

'Have you any orders for me?' asked Sassy.

'Yes I have,' replied Skeet firmly. 'Tam has prepared Thom's bunk for you for the time being, and it's time for you to use it.'

'But I'm not tired!'

'If you're going to be a sailor you must learn to sleep when you have the opportunity.'

'Skeet's right,' confirmed Jobey. 'You watch Pickle – he's a good example of that.'

The wind fell lighter as the twilight dimmed and Misty glided silently into the night. At midnight, Capt. Albern gave the order to alter course inshore, and Doc was secured to a line despite his protests. Tam commenced swinging the lead line, calling off the reading to Skeet, who hurried down the companionway to relay it to his skipper. Pickle, Chips and Waff stood at the ready among coils of running rigging awaiting orders, and Jobey concentrated on the compass, determined the needle would not waver a single degree from their course.

For three hours the crew worked tensely as Tam called off the depth. Sometimes the shore shelved more deeply and sometimes the water shoaled, and on each occasion Misty nudged closer inshore or veered away to sea as she felt her way through the dark. Tethered alone at the bow, Doc stared unblinkingly. He reflected that his task would be easier had not cloud obscured the moon. Even so he sensed the darker black of the forest slipping close by. He strained to catch the slightest sound, but all he could hear was the splash of the lead line and the occasional slap of a wavelet on Misty's hull.

Capt. Albern took a last look at the chart and climbed the companionway. 'We're nearly there,' he informed Skeet. 'There's a shallow spit just short of the entrance which we should be able to creep over. As soon as it deepens, we turn in. I'll take her now,' he said to Jobey, 'and well done.'

Jobey breathed a sigh of relief, glad to be relieved of the responsibility. He suddenly felt very tired and his legs wobbled as he made his way for'ard to help Skeet prepare the anchor.

'Three fathoms,' called Tam. Misty held her course.

'Two and shallowing!' he shouted.

'One!' he yelled urgently.

For what seemed an interminable time Misty crept on while the crew held their breath, dreading the lurch of the ship grounding.

'Two fathoms,' called Tam with relief. Capt. Albern allowed himself the flicker of a smile and turned his ship towards the shore.

'Trees!' squawked Doc in a panic.

'To port or starboard?' demanded Skeet, rushing to his side. Doc pointed into the inky black.

'Over there!'

'Land on the port bow,' called Skeet. Misty edged away.

'Now over there!' shouted Doc, stumbling across the deck and tripping over his lifeline.

'Land to starboard,' called Skeet.

Misty straightened up and ghosted into the creek, her crew peering into the dark on either side. Capt. Albern counted three minutes and gave the order to let go the anchor. It hit the water with a splash, the rattle of chain shattering the silence of the night. The sails furled and the ship made tidy, the crew gathered at the galley where The Cook handed out generous portions of soup.

'How about an extra ladle for those of us who did all the work?' suggested Pickle, nudging Chips and Waff, and with a sly glance at Jobey.

'I assume you're referring to Tam,' said Skeet.

'Tam as well as Chips, Waff and me.'

Tam rubbed his aching arm. 'Doc did his bit too. Where is he?'

'Come and get your soup, Doc,' called Skeet.

'Will someone please come and untie me,' came an exasperated voice from the bow. To everyone's surprise, Jobey put down his bowl and disappeared for'ard to release their disgruntled lookout.

'I reckon that's the hardest thing you've

done all night – leaning on that wheel watching us labour,' persisted Pickle. Jobey did not rise to the bait.

'It may interest you to know,' he replied, 'that the skipper said I did all right.' He then thanked The Cook for the very nice soup and fell asleep where he sat.

Tam and Skeet leaned on the rail while the crew made for their bunks.

'That was a fine piece of navigation. I'd be mighty pleased with myself if I was the skipper,' said Skeet with a yawn.

Tam stared into the dark. 'I'm glad he took the risk,' he said. 'I reckon they'll be here by morning – Thom's not far away.'

CHAPTER 15

Ancell struggled towards the ridge, Noname silently keeping pace. Leaving the glow of the fire below, they climbed beneath a myriad of stars twinkling in the velvet darkness of the desert night. Ancell limped badly, spasms of pain shooting up his leg at every step. He sensed Truegard willing him on, and looking up, saw a single star, shining more brightly than any other, and hanging so low above the ridge it seemed he could reach up and touch it if he could make the summit. Sometimes it span dizzily across the sky and Noname had to wait patiently at his side while he fought to bring it back into focus and climb again.

Their progress was agonisingly slow; so slow they were still fifty yards below the ridge top when dawn revealed the rocky crag above. Soon the light would expose the hillside and open them to view. Gritting his teeth, Ancell made a final effort, and hardly knowing what he was doing, clawed over the rim. He sank to the ground; then raised his head to gaze down on the valley. A few wisps of smoke drifted from the blackened earth, and flames still flickered in the compound, which resembled the remnants of an untidy bonfire. As he looked, a heavy timber burned through and collapsed in a shower of sparks.

Crawling the width of the narrow escarpment his heart leapt. In the distance rose the protection of a dense forest, already turning green in the strengthening light. Noname nudged him and pointed. A group of figures stood at the foot of two giant eucalyptus trees, waiting for a single straggler, who often stopped to look back.

Ancell sighed with relief. 'You see the tall figure,' he said. 'That's Jandamarra, the Aborigine who is our friend. The others are my shipmates and the children imprisoned with you. Once we get into the trees you'll be safe.' He glanced at the boy. He felt a closeness to him he did not understand.

'Why was it me you called?' he asked.

'Because if you survived that winter I thought you might help me,' said Noname.

Ancell recalled the first desperate year of his life. He had been born late in the summer with little time to eat and store sufficient fat to see him through a winter's hibernation, and as autumn drew in food had become harder to find. Weak and starving, he had lived only because someone had brought him milk and built him a shelter to protect him from the cold.

'It was you who saved my life?'

Noname nodded. 'I was in an orphanage, working in the fields, when I found you. They threw me out when they discovered I'd been stealing milk for you. I thought I'd go to sea and made for a port. Then Scarletta kidnapped me. When we landed here it was dark by the time we reached the camp and I managed to slip away, but they soon caught me. As a punishment I've been locked up day and night and fed only stale crusts and water. Some days there was no bread. Those were the days I thought you'd never come.'

Ancell recalled the times he had deserted the boy and bowed his head in shame.

'I should have come sooner,' he said. 'You've suffered so long for your kindness. I can never thank you enough.'

'You already have. You came,' said Noname – then clutched at Ancell fearfully at the sound of galloping horses.

'Keep low,' ordered Ancell, and they crawled back to peer down on five riders dismounting at the camp gate.

Laughing Jack glowered at the smouldering remains of the buildings.

'Those Aborigines will pay for this. I'll have every one of them hunted down,' he blazed.

'Forget them!' snapped Scarletta. 'It's Sassy

we want - and the other children if those animals got them out. You said the hedgehog was here when the gunpowder went up.'

'He was running towards the buildings when I first saw him. Then he collapsed. Maybe he'd been injured and was disorientated.'

'Or he was looking for the other child,' said Scarletta uneasily. Laughing Jack waved at the smoking ruins.

'The boy's probably under that lot - anyway they didn't know he was here.'

'But maybe the hedgehog did. That's why he's dangerous,' Scarletta murmured.

Larren's mind was fixed only on commanding Misty.

'If they did escape, the Aborigines will lead them to their ship,' he said. 'You need to attack before they sail or you'll lose all the children.'

Laughing Jack shrugged. 'We've time in hand. No one would risk sailing into that creek in the dark.'

'They might,' ventured Larren, mindful of Capt. Albern's mastery during the storm.

Laughing Jack mounted his horse. 'In which case we leave now; whatever they do they'll not escape me,' he growled.

Larren recalled Jandamarra's instruction to head for the ridge. If Ancell had been at the compound a few hours ago, alone and hurt, he would be easy prey. Presenting his dead body would earn him Laughing Jack's respect – apart from which, he despised the hedgehog almost as much as he had hated the red squirrel. He eyed Laughing Jack, bruised by the explosion and moving painfully.

'Maybe you should ride up that hill first in case you can see anyone,' he suggested.

Laughing Jack glared at him. 'I give the orders!' he rasped.

'It would be sensible,' said Scarletta.

'Then you go,' Laughing Jack ordered Larren. 'Go with him,' he instructed the two men. 'If he tries anything, shoot him.'

Larren suppressed a smile. Soon Misty would be within his grasp, but first he would have the pleasure of meeting Ancell for the last time.

Ancell breathed a sigh of relief as the riders set off into the desert. Then cold fear clutched at his heart as three peeled off to head towards the ridge. Larren was sitting astride the leading horse. He wanted to curl up and rest, but there was no hiding place. He wanted to run, but his leg made it impossible. He would have to face the grey squirrel. He led Noname back to within sight of the forest and took him by the shoulders.

'You must go on alone. Head for the two tall trees. Jandamarra will guide you to safety.'

Noname clutched him tightly.

Ancell pushed him away. 'Go! Keep your eyes on the trees and hurry!'

Reluctantly Noname started down the hillside, only to stop and look back.

'Go! I'll follow you,' shouted Ancell, and was relieved to see the boy scramble round an outcrop of rock and disappear from view.

He edged back to watch the riders. As the ground grew steeper the horses began to slip and he prayed they would give up and turn, but then he heard Larren call to the men to dismount and to follow him on foot. Seeking a place where Noname's path would be at Larren's back, he limped along the ridge to where a cliff fell sheer to a scree of broken rock far below. He felt perfectly calm now. His final task was to delay Larren long enough to give the boy a chance. He heard the laboured breathing of the climbing men – then looked into the pitiless eyes of the grey squirrel.

'Surprise, surprise!' mocked Larren. 'If it isn't the dreaming hedgehog, and all by himself! Too weak to keep up? Your honourable friends left you behind?'

'I'm waiting for you.'

'A big mistake, and your last.'

'I want to know what makes a traitor.'

Larren stiffened. 'Did you imagine I would put myself at risk for a few miserable children. Why should I care if they suffer? As for you, I despise your dreams. But you've served my purpose well and better still when you die.'

'And tell me what makes a coward,' said Ancell. 'Even now you can't face me without armed men at your side.'

Larren's eyes blazed and he kicked. The ferocious blow bowled Ancell over, but even as he lay gasping, the memory of that same kick at Truegard he had witnessed in the turmoil of the storm flashed into his consciousness. He understood now the grey squirrel's intent in the dark of that dreadful night. A raging anger welled in him as he staggered to his feet. Bent double with the searing pain at his ribs and fighting for breath, he limped towards Larren.

'You killed Truegard! You tried in the storm, even when he was risking his life to save yours! He didn't fall overboard – you murdered him!'

'The trusting Truegard, the trustworthy Truegard, the dependable first mate, loved and respected by captain and crew, who could always be relied upon to do his duty,' sneered Larren. 'Misty could never be mine with him on board.'

A terrible roaring engulfed Ancell's head, and in a mist of red he sprang at the grey squirrel's throat. He bit hard, and hung on as Larren twisted and turned to throw him off, unable to claw at his spines to prise him away.

'Kill him!' screamed Larren to the men.

The pirates raised their muskets, but so closely were the whirling animals entwined it was impossible to aim. One fired in the air in the hope Ancell would release his grip. Suddenly there was the sound of crumbling rock. Larren screamed, and Ancell felt himself falling. Instinctively he rolled into a ball. He fell for a long time before he hit the ground. He bounced, hit the ground again, bounced again and rolled to lay still.

The men peered over the cliff at the two lifeless bodies. They looked at each other, shrugged, and gathering the horses, rode away.

Ancell slipped in and out of consciousness. Sometimes he was on board Misty, feeling her comfortable pitch and roll. Sometimes he was in a far off country, resting beneath rustling beech trees and gazing over a patchwork of hedgerows and green fields. Then he felt the sun burning and recollected pitching over the cliff. Wincing at every movement, he uncurled. The forest lay below him, closer now, but beyond the limit of his strength. He lifted his head to the cliff to see Larren lying on his back, his head at a strange angle. He dragged himself closer. He had to be certain. Larren's body looked as fine and as powerful as ever, but the eyes stared unseeing directly into the glare of the sun. The grey squirrel was dead.

He felt no elation, only sadness at the loss of

Truegard's life. He slithered away from the corpse and took a last look at the trees protecting the children and his shipmates - the trees he would never reach. He whispered a thank you to Jandamarra, wished Misty God Speed, and drifted into sleep.

Jandamarra and Thom waited impatiently for Chad to catch up as the children and Merrie staggered into the forest.

'Get a move on!' called Thom.

Chad ignored her and again turned to stare back at the ridge. Jandamarra lost patience, and retracing his steps propelled the bosun into the trees.

'Why did you have to go so fast? I couldn't keep up,' growled Chad.

'Yes you could. You were hanging back for Ancell,' countered Thom mildly. 'Give him time - he's not the fastest of animals. We're close to Misty aren't we,' she said to Jandamarra.

'She may not even have reached the creek yet,' grumbled Chad.

'Yes she has. Tam's nearby,' said Thom.

Jandamarra pointed to a clearing where a stream bubbled.

'Not far now,' he said. 'You can drink and rest awhile now we're under cover. I'll watch for Ancell.'

Sinking gratefully to their knees, they drank

deeply. Jandamarra took a few sips and positioned himself with a view of the ridge. Chantal and Max slumbered and Merrie snored. Thom and Chad stretched out on their backs, feeling the warmth of the strengthening sun filter through the canopy of leaves high above.

'Sassy will be pleased to see Chantal and Max,' murmured Thom.

Chad rubbed his aching legs. 'And I'll be pleased to see my bunk. No more walking for me – ever!'

Then they heard the distant gunshot.

'Ancell!' gasped Chad, jumping to his feet and running to Jandamarra. 'Can you see anyone?' he demanded.

Jandamarra narrowed his eyes. A distant figure was stumbling towards them, though veering from side to side and close to walking in circles.

'There's a boy,' he said.

'Can you see Ancell?' asked Thom, joining them.

'The boy is alone. I'll fetch him.'

'Ancell's got to be with him,' argued Chad. 'He said he was going back for a child, so he must be. I'll come with you.'

'You won't be able to keep up, and anyway Laughing Jack's men may be following. I stand a better chance alone,' replied Jandamarra firmly.

Thom and Chad watched the Aborigine stride towards the ridge. Thom noticed his pace was double the speed they had walked. In the shimmering glare of sand and rock he seemed to glide above the ground.

Chad fidgeted. 'Ancell's out there somewhere. He might be wounded. I'm going after Jandamarra,' he said.

Jandamarra was already far distant.

'Can you move at that speed?' said Thom.

'No.'

'So we wait. The boy may be able to tell us something.'

Chad slumped against a tree. 'That madcap of a dreamer,' he muttered, 'I should never have left him alone.'

The sun was high before Jandamarra lifted the child from his back and set him down beside the stream.

Chad grabbed the boy. 'Where's Ancell?' he demanded. 'Has Laughing Jack got him? Who fired that shot?'

The boy cowered and buried his head in his arms. Thom pushed Chad aside.

'What's your name?' she asked gently.

'No name,' the boy whispered.

'Did a hedgehog rescue you?'

The head nodded.

'Do you know where he is?'

The exhausted boy looked up and Thom saw

the fear in his eyes. His lips struggled to speak.

'Hedgehog gone,' he eventually managed, and began to weep. Merrie started to cry and broke away from Chantal's comforting arm.

'I have to leave you now,' said Jandamarra sadly. 'I have little time to warn my people about the burning of the camp. Laughing Jack may take his revenge on our village. The stream will lead you to your ship.' He paused. 'You mourn for Ancell, but always remember he died on our sacred ground and his spirit will rest in peace.'

Chantal gave him a silent hug, and Max, Thom, Merrie and Chad shook his hand. Then he was gone as quickly and quietly as he had first appeared on the beach.

Thom lifted Noname onto her shoulders and they scrambled down the hillside. Suddenly, through the leaves of the trees below, they saw the glint of water and Misty lying peacefully at anchor. Thom pointed.

'My brother is on board. I bet he's the first to see us,' she said to Noname.

Noname struggled to be released and stood staring about wildly.

'Got to find the hedgehog,' he pleaded.

Chad edged up the hill. 'Don't you worry! I'm going to get him,' he called.

Thom walked towards the bosun. Chad, in turn, climbed a little higher.

'Use your sense,' said Thom. 'Get aboard first. Tam and I are fitter than you – if anyone goes back it should be us. The skipper will decide what to do.'

But Chad was well aware Capt. Albern was used to making hard decisions. The odds were that Ancell was dead, and the captain had the safety of his crew, the ship, and now the children to consider. However reluctantly, he would have to put to sea.

'Just ask the skipper to give me until nightfall,' he shouted, and walked away.

'We should stop him,' urged Chantal.

But Thom knew Chad, and with an exasperated sigh, took Noname's hand and started for the creek.

CHAPTER 16

Tam slept briefly and was already on deck at first light, certain that Thom was drawing closer. He gave a low whistle of amazement as he looked about him. A bend in the creek hid the open sea and Misty appeared to be landlocked. All around, the forest sloped steeply to the water, birds rustled in the tops of trees towering high above Misty's masts, and along the muddy shore a tangle of mangroves swayed silently in the barely perceptible heave of the unseen ocean swell.

Capt. Albern appeared and sent for Pickle and Jobey to row him to the entrance of the inlet to confirm the ship was truly hidden. Skeet and Tam helped lower the gig and turned their attention to Doc, who was repeatedly tossing a bucket on a length of line over the side.

'It's to attract crocodiles,' explained Doc.

'I'm not sure crocodiles eat buckets,' said Tam.

'Of course they don't,' retorted Doc, 'but the splashing makes them curious. Don't you want to see one? I've read they can grow to a length of thirty feet.'

'In which case I'd prefer we don't arouse their interest,' stated Skeet, watching the gig, which suddenly looked very small. 'Put it back in the bosun's locker before you have to answer to Chad for losing it.'

Pickle and Jobey considered the skipper made them row further than necessary before ordering their return. It was hard work in the sultry air, and the captain frowned as the boat slowed.

'Put some effort into it!' puffed Pickle.

'It's you that's not pulling your weight,' grunted Jobey, heaving mightily, but the gig had come to a halt.

'Why don't you look where you're going?' complained a nasal voice at the bow.

The sailors span round to see close by and just above the waterline, a glaring pair of eyes, and closer still, a jaw of formidable teeth and the end of a snout. At that moment Jobey knew he was about to be eaten by a very large crocodile. All the grievous misfortunes he had suffered and every indignity he had endured flashed before him. Fate had never looked upon him kindly. His cup had never been anywhere near half full. If it was not one thing it was another. It was altogether too much. He stood up, and raising his oar high above his head, whacked the crocodile on the nose.

'Why don't you get out of the way!' he yelled.

The gig rocked, Jobey sat down quickly, and the eyes appeared alongside.

'Temper! Temper!' chided the crocodile.

Pickle began to talk very fast in a high-pitched voice.

'Please accept our abject apologies, kind Sir,' he pleaded. 'We were careless in the extreme, though to be honest it was more the fault of Jobey here than me. We are but poor ignorant sailors, nothing but skin and bone as you see, but if you would allow us to return to our ship, we have a very fine cook on board, the most excellent of cooks, who would make you a very good breakfast.'

'Would that be what he cooks or the cook himself?' enquired the crocodile.

'May I introduce myself,' intervened Capt. Albern quickly. 'I am the master of "Misty Dawn". Please forgive our intrusion, but we wish to collect our crew who are fleeing for their lives. If we fail they will almost certainly be shot.'

The eyes submerged and surfaced by the captain.

'And do you carry firearms?' asked the crocodile.

'Certainly not!'

'I'm glad to hear it.'

'May we have your permission to take them on board?'

The crocodile took his time considering. 'It'll cost you an arm and a leg,' he replied.

There was silence in the gig. 'Only joking,' sighed the crocodile.

'And if there's anything we can do for you, we will,' offered Pickle.

'As it happens there is. I've recently had to warn off a couple of sharks that were trespassing on my territory, and they've left a whole lot of teeth in my belly. They itch, and I'd appreciate you taking them out.'

At that moment, a sea eagle swooped low above the crocodile, who heaved himself half out of the water, made a belated and half-hearted attempt to snap at the bird, and flopped back with a mighty splash. Morosely he watched the bird soar over the treetops.

'She does that to annoy me,' he said with an air of resignation. 'But in a few years she'll not be as fast as she thinks, and then I'll have her. I do apologise! I've made you all wet.'

'Not at all! Beautifully refreshing!' spluttered Pickle, jabbing Jobey in the ribs.

'Delightfully cooling!' added Jobey quickly.

'See you at the ship,' said the crocodile, and with the faintest of ripples glided for Misty.

'You should watch your manners – attacking innocent creatures like that,' Pickle reproved Jobey.

'Oh Mr Crocodile Sir!' Jobey mimicked

Pickle's quavering voice. 'It's all my shipmate's fault. Eat him, not me.'

'Stop bickering and row,' ordered Capt. Albern, wringing the water from his cap and wondering how to persuade Waff, for it would be the job of the sailmaker, to operate on so fearsome a beast. His thoughts were interrupted by seeing the crocodile, thrashing wildly with his tail, rise three quarters of his length from the churning water, claw onto Misty's bulwarks, and remarkably quickly heave his bulk on board. He also watched his crew and Sassy scamper equally as fast high up the rigging.

Doc, stepping on deck after searching his cabin for a book about swamps in general and the properties of mangrove seeds in particular, was the first to make the acquaintance of the newcomer.

'Wonderful!' he exclaimed. 'What an honour and a pleasure to meet you Sir. Beaufoy is the name, Dr Eugene Beaufoy.'

'Hector,' replied the crocodile.

'I've been trying to attract you.'

'Was it you banging that bucket in the water?'

'Indeed it was.'

Hector glowered. 'Well don't!' he grumbled. 'Have you no idea how much noise it makes! First you wake me up in the middle of the night heaving anchors overboard, and then you interrupt my morning nap. Incidentally, do the crew normally sit in the rigging?'

Doc surveyed the near thirty feet of Hector's scaly body, the podgy legs, the clawed feet, the hooded eyes and the rows of well-worn teeth.

'They're a bit nervous. You do look...how shall I put it...quite formidable.'

'Do you really think so?'

'I think you're magnificent!'

'You're too kind! Of course I'm at my most graceful in the water,' said Hector, closing his eyes bashfully and demurely curling his tail round the mast.

Capt. Albern signalled his reluctant crew to return to the deck and insisted every one of them present themselves. Sassy managed only a gulp, and the portly Chips twisted his bowler before him as he told of his poverty stricken widowed mother, who depended upon him for a few crusts. Hector held court with an occasional grunt of acknowledgment, but more often in silence, holding his jaw wide open. This, Doc enlightened the sailors, was to cool him, and suggested his friend would appreciate some shade, as too much heat might make him irritable. The crew glanced at one another, and very quickly erected a tarpaulin, adjusting the canopy upwards and downwards, forwards and backwards, and from one side to the other, until Hector confirmed the temperature was exactly to his liking.

Capt. Albern strode back and forth on the afterdeck, the sailmaker and the carpenter standing with bowed heads before him. Waff had argued fiercely that cutting and sewing crocodile stomachs was far beyond his duties either as sailmaker or unofficial ship's medic. Chips, who the captain had suggested should assist, agreed he would do the job if Hector were a wooden crocodile – but he wasn't. The two craftsmen stared defiantly at the deck whilst their skipper pondered.

'Doc!' they exclaimed as one.

'There's probably a special technique for crocodiles, and he's bound to know it,' reasoned Waff.

'And Hector seems to like him, so he's less likely to eat him,' added Chips.

Doc was summoned and informed that the combination of his intelligence and the shape of his beak made him the ideal candidate. Doc looked at them with mild surprise and replied that Hector had already asked, and if they'd excuse him he'd like to get on with the job.

Hector rolled onto his back to display his ample stomach, and Misty's crew suddenly found tasks requiring urgent attention at the far ends of the ship. The Cook beckoned Skeet to the galley.

'What am I to give him for lunch?' he whispered.

'I'm sure he'll enjoy whatever you make.'

'But what if he doesn't? What then?'

'The Cook is asking what you'd like for lunch,' called Skeet to Hector from behind the galley door.

'Couldn't touch a thing. I ate a couple of months ago, but thank you for asking,' replied the crocodile.

The Cook sank to his knees and gave thanks.

Doc worked purposefully, extracting the shark teeth from the soft white skin criss-crossed with scars.

'You've taken a good number of bites over the years,' he observed, tossing a tooth over his shoulder.

'I make sure everybody knows the creek is my patch,' grunted Hector.

'I've read that your flesh heals itself when you're wounded.'

'We learned to do that long ago. Common sense I'd say.'

Doc paused from pecking and adjusted his pince-nez. 'This looks like a gunshot wound.'

Hector sighed. 'Men,' he said. 'Now they've got guns they seem determined to kill us for some reason, despite the fact this is our home and we existed millions of years before they even evolved. Three thousand years ago the pharaohs worshipped us, but ever since it's been downhill all the way for us crocodiles.'

'I should warn you that armed men might follow my shipmates here.'

'Which is why I'll help you all I can.'

Doc dropped the last of the teeth on the deck. 'All done!' he announced.

'Very kind of you,' yawned Hector. 'Now if you'll excuse me I think I'll take a nap.'

'I'll tell everyone not to make a noise,' said Doc.

Hector was immediately awoken by a shout from the crowsnest.

'Ahoy there!' yelled Tam, seeing his sister step from the undergrowth and answering her distant hail. The crew almost forgot about Hector as they rushed to the side to wave as the rescue party emerged from the jungle.

'Looks like they've a girl and a couple of boys with them,' said Chips.

'They've rescued Chantal and Max!' cried Sassy with delight.

'Can't see Chad or Ancell yet,' said Jobey.

'Can Tam and I take the gig? We can pick all of them up in a couple of trips,' Skeet asked Capt. Albern.

'Please can I go ashore, I want to collect some mangrove seeds,' pleaded Doc.

Not having the heart to refuse yet another of the owl's requests, especially after his valiant efforts on Hector's stomach, the sea otter consented. Everyone watched Skeet and Tam pull for the shore, Doc sitting proudly in the stern, determined to make the most of his opportunity to explore.

Laughing Jack and Scarletta, stooping low, crept towards the creek, followed by two men, their muskets at the ready. Scarletta pointed through the trees.

'There!' she whispered.

Laughing Jack stared down on Misty lying peacefully at anchor. 'Here so soon!' he muttered.

As they watched, a rowing boat appeared from behind the ship and headed for the far shore. Scarletta pushed a branch aside, and catching sight of Thom and the children waiting at the water's edge, gripped Laughing Jack's arm.

'Just in time,' she murmured.

'Got you! You've walked right back into my hands! As for you animals – you're dead!' snarled Laughing Jack, brandishing his gun and beginning to laugh. The trigger-happy pirates, knowing the captain's laughter was a certain signal to kill, levelled their muskets at the boat and fired. In an apoplexy of fury Laughing Jack knocked the men to the ground, but not before he glimpsed the children disappear into the trees.

'Now we'll have to flush them out,' he seethed.

'But what if they have the Aborigines with them? Do you want to fight them in the forest where we can't see them,' countered Scarletta, watching the rowing boat quickly head back behind the protection of Misty's hull. 'They'll have to pick them up sooner or later, so we stick to our original plan. We watch, and as soon as they've ferried the children on board we send in the canoes to attack before they sail. They'll probably wait until nightfall now, but there'll be moon enough to see.'

'And those Aborigines will only be able to watch,' agreed Laughing Jack.

Misty's crew stared about in disbelief as the gunfire reverberated across the creek.

'Anyone see where the shots came from?' asked Capt. Albern grimly. Nobody had.

'They were quite distant,' said Pickle. 'We'd be out of range so they were probably firing at the gig. Skeet and Tam are rowing back.'

'Out of range or not, I bet I'm the next target,' grumbled Jobey.

Onshore, Thom quickly led the terrified children, closely followed by Merrie, into deep cover.

'Laughing Jack's followed us. We must run,' begged Chantal.

Thom held her back, sensing the closer they stayed to Misty the better their chances.

'The gunfire came from the end of the creek,'

she argued. 'The light will have gone before they'd be able to reach us and they've no chance of finding us in the dark. Tam won't leave without me, and Misty won't sail without us – the skipper will come up with something.'

'And Chad said he'd be back tonight,' added Merrie.

Skeet and Tam pulled hard for Misty. Doc groaned.

'Are you all right?' asked Skeet, as the boat nosed alongside the ship. One of the shots had been close enough to splinter his oar.

'I've been wounded,' moaned Doc.

Skeet inspected the trickle of blood tinging the feathers above the owl's left eye.

'You're lucky, Doc. It's just a graze,' he said.

'Mortally wounded I fear,' stated Doc, who then insisted he was weakening fast and demanded to be hauled up in a bosun's chair.

Waff was called. 'Nothing more than a scratch,' he announced.

'I'm dying,' whispered Doc.

Waff sighed. 'In that case I'll have to operate.' He grinned. 'Of course I'll have to pluck you first.'

Doc glared at the sailmaker. 'That will not be necessary,' he replied firmly. 'I prefer to pass from this world in peace and in one piece.'

'Stop making such a fuss!' grumbled Jobey.

'That'll teach you to keep your head down,' said Pickle.

'Remember me,' whispered Doc, and closed his eyes.

'You are not dying!' stated Skeet irritably.

'Farewell,' murmured Doc, and striking the pose of a fallen hero, lay his head on an outstretched wing, only opening one eye at intervals in sad contemplation of his shipmates. Eventually Hector heaved himself alongside the casualty and ordered a strip of his flesh to be bound to the wound to ensure it healed cleanly. A nod from Capt. Albern told Waff there was no argument this time. Hector rolled over, and with a deep breath the sailmaker sliced a slither from his belly.

'Finished?' asked Hector, but Waff had already sprung behind the protection of the mast.

'I don't think I'll ever forgive you for this,' he quietly advised Doc, as he bandaged the owl's head.

'Thanks Hector! I feel better already!' called Doc, looking about him. 'There's not many who can say they owe their life to a crocodile,' he proudly informed the crew, and to Waff's fury, stood up unaided.

Capt. Albern and Skeet stood on the afterdeck, debating how to rescue the search party.

'We've got to act fast before they're found,' argued Skeet. 'If I lay in the bottom of the gig I'd be protected, and I could still row.'

Capt. Albern shook his head. 'They're safer in the forest. Take a boat now and it will be riddled with fire.'

'But what if they're forced to flee again? Then we won't know where they are.'

'Tam!' called Capt. Albern. 'What's Thom most likely to do?'

'She's staying close by and hiding until dark,' said Tam.

'Then we'll wait for dark too,' Capt. Albern told Skeet, and made his way for'ard. He coughed discreetly to wake Hector who was dozing peacefully.

'Thank you for sorting out Doc,' he said.

'Think nothing of it,' replied the crocodile, opening one eye. 'What are you going to do now?'

'I'll try sending a boat as soon as it's dark – the trouble is there's a moon. Any ideas?'

Hector ruminated. 'A boat will be seen. I'll pick them up myself.'

'Carry them on your back?'

'That would make them an easy target. Anyway they'd probably fall off. Much safer to ferry them in my mouth.'

Capt. Albern remembered the ability of a crocodile to pick up an egg without cracking the shell, but still hesitated.

'Isn't that...well...a bit risky.'

'Have no fears, I'll demonstrate,' said Hector with a wink. 'Hey you! Fatty!' he called to Chips.

'Me?' quavered the carpenter.

'Yes you!' cried the rest of the crew.

'There's nothing to worry about,' insisted Capt. Albern. 'Hector wishes to show us how he will rescue the search party.'

'Why me?' faltered Chips, looking for a way of escape, but with a twist of his tail Hector was already at his side.

'Because there's a lot of you,' answered Waff with delight.

'Step inside,' invited Hector, and opened his mouth.

'I refuse to be demonstrated on,' protested Chips, but with a flick of his head Hector closed his jaws about the carpenter, raised him high, and paraded him from side to side for everyone to view. After a round of applause, Chips was returned to the deck, where he stood for a moment clutching his bowler before his legs gave way. Hector, however, had not finished.

'Gentlemen!' he addressed his audience, 'you have just witnessed the sensitivity of a crocodile. Now behold what many have experienced, but none have lived to tell the tale.' He raised his head, slowly opened his jaws, then in a flash, shut them with such a clunk Misty's timbers shivered.

'The weight of that was more than two thousand pounds per square inch,' he pronounced, and waited until Capt. Albern perceptively commenced another round of applause. Inwardly, the crew shuddered, none more so than Chips.

'Sheer exhibitionism,' he grumbled to Waff. 'And he's got bad breath - almost as bad as yours.'

CHAPTER 17

Chad tramped for the distant ridge, feeling very exposed but ignoring the possibility of being seen. Gasping for breath, he stumbled on until at last the ground began to rise, and glancing up, saw a bird gliding above the crag. As he watched, it was joined by another, and then another.

'Vultures!' he muttered, and redoubled his efforts. The birds circled slowly lower, biding their time, until the first landed at the foot of the cliff. Chad climbed more furiously.

'Clear off!' he yelled, hurling a stone at it. The vulture stood its ground and Chad saw at its feet the twisted body of Larren, his neck clearly broken. Not giving the grey squirrel a second glance, he scrambled higher, and missing a foothold set off a small avalanche of scree. Silently cursing as he paused for breath, he watched the debris tumble down the slope to hit a rounded stone - which twitched.

'Ancell!' he cried, and slithered down to the hedgehog.

Ancell stuck out his head.

'Am I glad to see you,' he whispered.

Chad held a flask of water to Ancell's lips. 'Are you hurt?' he asked.

'My leg's painful. I tripped in the compound. Thanks for coming back.'

'I assumed you'd do something stupid like falling over.'

'Have you got Noname?'

'Thanks to you he'll be safely on board by now.'

Ancell drank deeply, feeling a little strength returning, and more hopeful now that Chad was at his side. He passed back the flask.

'Larren's dead.'

Chad nodded. 'So I saw. We heard gunfire and thought you'd been shot. Did Laughing Jack kill him?'

'He fell off the ridge with me.'

Chad stared up at the cliff. 'You fell from there!'

'All the way.'

The rat glanced at the body of Larren and spoke gravely with heavy emphasis.

'Listen carefully. You must understand that you are hurt more seriously than you realise. I'll go for a stretcher party. Meanwhile, sip the water, try to stay awake, and don't attempt to move.'

'Stop wittering and help me up. Hedgehogs bounce – all I've got is a few bruises.'

'That's not possible!'

'It's true. Our spines have a special honeycomb structure which makes them exceptionally strong and flexible.'

Chad looked up at the ridge again and whistled.

'Some bounce!' he declared, and carefully lifted Ancell to his feet. They took a final look at the body of the grey squirrel.

'Take a peck for me!' yelled Chad to the vultures.

Ancell leaned heavily on Chad's shoulder as they shuffled for the cool of the forest, Chad telling Ancell what a foolhardy, blithering idiot he was to take such a risk alone, that he could not be left for a moment without finding trouble, and moreover that if he followed his visions with a little more care and a little less fighting it would save them all a lot of bother – and Ancell reminding Chad that he could think of no one less qualified to lecture about getting into fights, that only the most stubborn of fools would risk his life turning back for him, and furthermore that whilst a tail on board a ship was no doubt useful, it hardly compared to a good set of spines when it came to falling off cliffs.

Thom watched the last of the daylight fade from above the forest canopy. Beneath the trees it was already dark as she led the way to the edge of the creek. Rising above the forest, the moon bathed Misty in a pool of light, her silhouette stark and clear on the silver water. Anxiously they looked for signs of rescue.

'Is anyone coming?' whispered Chantal.

'Not yet, but they will,' Thom assured her, but she felt a sense of disquiet as she surveyed the dark outline of the far shore where she was certain the gunmen were watching. A boat would be seen easily, and they stood little more chance of getting on board than in broad daylight.

'Compliments of the captain to you,' came a deep voice from the water's edge.

'Who's that!' stammered Thom, pushing the children and Merrie behind her.

'And don't panic and start crashing about or you'll wake half the neighbourhood,' instructed the voice.

'Where are you? Show yourself!' demanded Thom, staring about.

'I'll come ashore then,' grunted Hector.

The children clasped their hands to their mouths, Merrie uttered a small squeak, and Thom stood transfixed as the crocodile slid from the water, heaved his body clear of the ground, and at a sedate pace, waddled towards them.

'I'm Hector, and I assume you're Thom. I've already had the pleasure of meeting your brother,' he addressed the field mouse. Thom blanched.

'He's asked me to assure you, quite unnecessarily in my view, that you'll be quite safe with me,' added the crocodile.

Thom relaxed. 'We're waiting to be picked up,' she said.

'Which is why I'm here,' replied Hector. 'Now who's first? The sooner I've ferried you on board the sooner I can get some sleep.'

'I'll go,' offered Thom. 'What do I do?'

'Just relax,' yawned Hector, and in a single movement flopped to his belly, picked up the field mouse and slid into the creek. Thom felt Hector's jaws hold her firmly as the silky water momentarily closed over her. She surfaced with a splutter to find herself propelled powerfully and silently towards Misty. Within minutes Hector was nosing her to the foot of the rope ladder hanging from the ship's side. She clasped a rung and climbed into the embrace of Tam.

'Good trip?' asked Tam with a grin.

'Amazing! I must speak to the skipper.'

'Welcome aboard,' called Capt. Albern.

The crew encircling Thom parted as the captain stepped forward. Thom was brief and to the point. They had rescued a girl and two boys. Ancell was almost certainly dead, and they had lost Chad. The sailors bowed their heads in heavy silence. The death of Ancell would not leave the hole in their lives that Truegard's did, but the loss of the strange hedgehog they had once considered nothing more than a passenger but had almost become one of them, came as a shock. He was not the sort of animal to die in a fight, and they wondered sadly what accident had befallen him. The probable loss of Chad was devastating. They had always assumed the bosun to be imperishable, often bloodied but always surviving to fight another day. Sailing without him was unthinkable even though they knew they should flee the moment the children were on board.

'And Chad definitely said he'd be back by nightfall?' questioned Capt. Albern.

Thom nodded miserably. It was the third time the skipper had asked. She thought the old sea otter looked greyer than ever as he paced the afterdeck, his head bowed.

'Please can someone give me a hand?' called Max, clinging to the top of the ladder.

'Welcome aboard,' said Thom, hauling him on board. 'Everyone! This is Max.'

But even as Misty's crew jostled each other to introduce themselves, Max was running to Sassy.

'Introductions later,' Skeet ordered the crew, and ushered the two children to Truegard's cabin. Leaving them talking excitedly, he paused outside the door. Nobody had suggested or even considered using the empty cabin until now. He missed the red squirrel's gentle reminders, promptings and cautionary advice as much as ever, and sometimes when off duty, restless and unable to sleep, he had sat there, feeling Truegard's calm reassurance. He suspected the skipper had too. Through the door he heard Sassy chuckling and a peal of laughter from Max. Truegard, he thought, would be pleased.

Chantal asked Hector to ferry Noname next. He curled between Hector's jaws and shut his eyes. He only opened them when Tam, hanging at the bottom of the ladder, wrapped an arm round him and lifted him on board.

Chantal and Merrie huddled close, feeling even more isolated. The girl felt Merrie shiver, and although she dreaded the wait alone, told him to go first. Merrie had been imagining a hero's welcome, but then remembered he would have to face The Cook, and decided the encounter was best delayed for as long as possible.

'You go, I wouldn't want to leave you by yourself,' he replied gallantly. 'Chantal's next,' he told Hector, as the crocodile slid silently from the water.

Hector frowned at Merrie. 'You're a problem. There's nothing of you to get a grip. You'd better lie between my eyes while I take Chantal.'

'It would be more fun to ride right up front on the end of your snout,' said Merrie.

'Certainly not! Do as you're told,' grumbled Hector, adding that for an unnaturally small animal the harvest mouse was extremely precocious, to which Merrie replied he was not only that but a sailor and trekker as well.

Truegard's increasingly crowded cabin was soon filled with excited chatter as Max and Chantal, talking at the same time, questioned Sassy about her time with the Aborigines, and Sassy interrogated them about the fire and their escape. Noname shook Sassy's hand and retreated to a corner.

It was quieter in the fo'c'sle. Thom added a few cursory details of their imprisonment and Jandamarra's rescue, confirming, as they all now knew, that they were facing men who would not hesitate to kill. Chips started to tell Thom how Hector had chosen him above all others to demonstrate the rescue, but his heart was not in the story, and lacking even the briefest riposte from Waff, lapsed into silence. They were all thinking of Chad. It seemed Ancell's fate was sealed, but there was still the possibility the bosun could be alive, and even at that moment struggling for the safety of the ship.

'I'm glad I'm not the skipper,' muttered Jobey, and everyone nodded in silent agreement.

Alone in the dark, the sea otter wrestled with his thoughts. The right decision was undoubtedly to up anchor. The remaining hours of darkness offered Misty her best chance of escape and the children their freedom. Even so he was loath to give the order to sail. He made his way for'ard to Skeet and Hector.

'We'll wait until the very last moment – just before dawn,' he informed Skeet.

'Hector could take me ashore to look for him,' offered the second mate.

The sea otter shook his head. 'If I thought you'd be able to see anything I'd send you willingly, but it will be pitch dark under the trees.'

'I'll hear anyone a lot easier without you crashing about,' said Hector, and without another word slipped over the side.

Merrie drew a deep breath and poked his head round the galley door.

'I'm sorry!' he said, shifting uneasily from one leg to another.

The Cook paused from stirring a pot – then started stirring again.

'I left you a message,' offered Merrie.

But The Cook's mind was elsewhere. He pushed the pot to the back of the stove and leaned on the ship's rail, staring darkly at the shore.

'There's some soup ready,' he eventually said. 'Take it to the children and don't spill it.'

Chad and Ancell, breathing hard, spoke less and less as they journeyed painfully through the evening. Using the rat as a crutch, Ancell trod awkwardly, often causing Chad to stumble, when they would be forced to stop and cling together dizzy with fatigue until they regained their balance. Twice, the legs of the weary rat buckled, and he silently cursed them for giving way. He watched their shadows lengthen, and as he had long feared, knew they would not reach the creek before nightfall. Concentrating on the two tall trees, he staggered on faster, praying his skipper would risk granting him a little more time. The moon rose and they shuffled on through the night, tiring with every step, until at last they collapsed into the forest.

'Got to rest!' pleaded Ancell.

Chad glanced back, and realised with a dreadful despair that he could make out the top of the ridge, not by moonlight but by the first light of the new day.

'No time!' he urged, and ignoring Ancell's whimpers of pain, half dragged him towards the creek, only to trip over a log, pulling the half sobbing hedgehog on top of him. They rolled free of each other to look into a reproachful pair of eyes.

'Amazing! Your shipmates don't look where they're going on water, and you don't on land. I come to look for you and you walk all over me,' grumbled Hector.

Chad gulped and looked wildly to Ancell,

but the hedgehog had already curled into a ball.

'Is your companion shy or just plain rude?' enquired Hector.

'He's a bit stupid that way,' stammered Chad, feeling for a stick and poking Ancell hard. 'Please don't eat us,' he begged.

Hector sighed. 'Eating is all you rodents seem to think about. I need to get you on board before daylight, and that means now. Please tell your friend to unravel himself.'

Ancell, who had gathered the gist of the conversation, risked poking out his nose.

'Thank you!' acknowledged Hector with heavy sarcasm. 'Follow me, and try to make less noise.'

To Hector's irritation there was further delay at the waters edge, when he explained they were to be transported by mouth. Chad told Ancell he had volunteered him to go first, which Ancell said he did not recall hearing, to which Chad retorted he would have done if he hadn't rolled up. Eventually Hector lost patience, and with the threat of leaving them where they were, instructed both of them to lie across his jaw. Ancell was additionally informed that if he raised a single spine he would immediately be dropped off. He lay very still.

'The things I do for you!' Chad muttered from the corner of his mouth as they cruised through the water, but feeling a warning increase of pressure from Hector's teeth, said not another word.

Misty's crew tumbled joyfully from the fo'c'sle as Skeet shouted the news they had hardly dare hope for. Doc hurried from his bunk, and in his excitement bumped his head on the cabin roof. Capt. Albern offered a prayer of thanks and left his lonely vigil at the stern, and The Cook shuffled from the galley with two mugs of hot drink. Disobeying orders to remain below, the children joined in the melee about the two heroes, and Hector added to the confusion by hauling himself on board to take up most of the space on deck. Chad managed a weak grin as Capt. Albern stepped forward.

'Thanks for waiting, Skipper.'

The sea otter shrugged. 'You'd better get some rest. We're sailing this moment,' he replied. Ancell thought he saw a tear of relief in the captain's eye as he turned away.

Hector raised his head. 'As it appears you no longer require my services, and if no one has anything further to say, I'll be going,' he sniffed, and turning his back, huffily lurched to the ship's side.

Capt. Albern acted quickly. 'Gentlemen!' he called. 'We have assembled here, not only to welcome our shipmates aboard, but also to pay tribute to one we hold in high esteem. Hector, you have saved many lives, perhaps all our lives. We applaud your courage, we pay homage to your prowess, and we thank you for your friendship.'

Hector bowed his head graciously to an enthusiastic round of applause, and manoeuvred himself back to centre stage.

'Thank you indeed! Thank you all,' he responded, rather more happily. 'May I in turn wish Misty a safe and speedy passage home.'

'Come with us!' shouted Doc from the back of the crowd, causing Capt. Albern a moment of panic. But Hector shook his head and told the owl that the creek had always been good enough for him, and there was a lot to be said for staying in one's own back yard. Sassy and Chantal ran forward to give him a kiss, and Hector lay for a moment, blushing and displaying a silly lopsided smile, then with a flick of his tail slid over the side. For a brief moment everyone watched an arrow shaped ripple glide through the water, and then he was gone.

Hector's departure jolted everyone back to reality. The light was fast strengthening and soon Misty would be in full view of the watching gunmen. Chips and Waff slid a screen of planking behind the wheel to protect the helmsman, and the children were sent to their cabin.

'And you, Merrie,' ordered Skeet.

Merrie was about to argue, but caught The Cook's warning eye, and stomped below.

Capt. Albern took the helm, and at his nod the fore-spencer and foresails were hoisted. Then the crew scrambled aft to raise the main and the gaff-topsail, then dashed for'ard again to weigh anchor.

'Heave, two, three, heave!' urged Skeet, as he leant his weight to their efforts. Slowly the capstan turned and the chain clanked over Misty's bow.

'They'll hear this!' grunted Jobey, waiting for the deck to be raked by fire.

'Heave for your life then,' puffed Pickle.

At last Misty gave a shiver of excitement as the anchor broke from the mud. They left it hanging above the water and scampered aloft to unfurl the topsail and topgallant, then scuttled under the protection of the bulwarks. In the still of the early morning the sails hung limp, but Capt. Albern waited patiently, glad he had insisted every last barnacle had been chipped from her planking when she was beached. With a clean hull she would soon come alive to the faintest of the zephyrs he sensed moving high above her deck, and already the slight current of the streams tumbling into the creek was drawing her seaward. Skeet scurried aft to join him.

'So far, so good, Mr Skeet,' allowed the skipper. Skeet watched the distance from the shore slowly widen.

'Not a single shot,' he said. 'I reckon those gunmen have gone.'

'It'll be a while before we see blue water,' warned the captain. 'But I must say everything seems very satisfactory, very satisfactory indeed.'

CHAPTER 18

Scarletta tensed at the rattle of Misty's anchor chain and urgently shook Laughing Jack awake.

'I don't understand. They're leaving without the children,' she said.

Laughing Jack rubbed the sleep from his eyes and cursed.

'Seems like they're ditching them - and some of their crew. No doubt they've decided to run for their own lives,' he muttered. 'I'll have the men flush the children out later, but first I want to see that ship go down.' He kicked the two sleeping pirates awake.

'Join the boarding party,' he ordered. 'Offer the crew their lives for the girl. Once she's in your hands, shoot every one of those animals and scuttle the ship.'

Misty's crew fidgeted impatiently, willing her to pick up speed. Their hearts lifted as the sea opened into view, only to sink when two canoes appeared from behind the headland. Each boat carried six men. Two paddled hard and four crouched low, holding muskets to their shoulders. The canoes slowed within hailing distance.

'Heave to! We're coming aboard,' bellowed a pirate. Capt. Albern motioned Skeet to take the helm and marched to the rail. All he could do was to play for time and pray for a wind.

'Identify yourselves!' he demanded.

'Don't fool with us! You have Sassy on board,' shouted the pirate. 'Hand her over and you can go. Either that or we kill you.'

'There's no girl on board this ship. Come and see for yourselves,' invited the captain, and issued a stream of urgent orders. Tam and Thom dropped two rope ladders to just high enough above the water to make them difficult to grasp. Pickle crouched below the bulwarks at the for'ard one, armed with a heavy length of chain, and Chips crawled to his side with an axe. Hidden at the aft ladder, Jobey nursed the weight of a crowbar and Waff gripped a viciously serrated knife.

Misty slipped along a little faster to meet the swell of the open sea, her gentle rolling making it more difficult for the canoes to lie alongside, but even so the first of the pirates eventually clung to the ladders and began to climb.

'Get more of you on the ladder. The heavier it is the less it will swing about,' advised Tam, and was pleased to see more men follow the leading pair.

The first man arrived at the rail. Pickle struck, and with two quick swings of the axe,

Chips cut the ladder free. Simultaneously, Jobey leaned over the aft ladder to cosh the leading man's wrist. Waff's knife flashed, and the ladder tumbled away. Shouting and cursing, the men pitched onto those climbing below, and struggling to disentangle themselves from the ladders, they all tumbled back into the wildly lurching canoes.

'Bye-bye!' yelled Pickle.

'You can keep the ladders!' mocked Chips. But everyone knew their assailants would be back.

'Come on wind!' pleaded Skeet, handing the helm back to his skipper, but cruelly the little breeze there was faltered and died.

Ancell awoke from a deep sleep at the clamour of the boarding party and dragging himself on deck found Chad digging weapons from the bosun's locker – lengths of chain, two boathooks, and spare belaying pins.

'Never give up,' instructed the rat, handing him a length of heavy piping.

'Go for their throats!' exhorted Skeet, practicing using a boathook as a lance.

Ancell took his place at the rail. At his side stood Chad, who no more than hours ago had saved his life, and was now specifying in graphic terms the bloodcurdling injuries he was about to inflict. Tam and Thom stood shoulder-to-shoulder, waiting quietly, while Skeet paced impatiently back and forth. Chips was extolling the virtues of an axe as a weapon. Waff gripped a belaying pin while puffing furiously on his pipe. Jobey glowered and Pickle whistled defiantly as they swung crowbars menacingly. The Cook limped from the galley, armed with a meat cleaver and clenching a carving knife between his teeth, and Capt. Albern stood resolutely at the helm, gently easing the wheel a few spokes one way and then the other to catch the elusive breath of air they so desperately needed.

'Here they come,' muttered Chad.

The assault was better prepared this time. One canoe stood off a little, a line of muskets trained on Misty. The other paddled close alongside, the men swinging grappling irons and climbing nets. It would be easy for them, Ancell realised, just a matter of time before the marksmen picked off Misty's crew as they showed themselves to fight off the boarding party. Tears clouded his eyes. His quest had already cost Truegard his life, and now the children would suffer once more and Misty's decks run with the blood of her crew. He wondered if Merrie could hide. He feared Doc, sent below with the children, would stand no chance.

'Down everybody!' shouted Skeet.

Splinters of wood flew from the bulwarks as

the first volley struck. Capt. Albern crouched at the helm, still searching for a whisper of wind.

For a long tense minute everyone waited in silence for the first of the grappling irons to thud on board. Suddenly they heard screams of terror, and daring to peer above the bulwarks, stood open mouthed. One canoe was upside down, its crew floundering in the water. Then they saw Hector clamp his jaws onto the other. His white belly flashed and plumes of spray rose high in the air as he thrashed the sea to drag it over. A man pointed a pistol, but with a flick of his tail Hector knocked him overboard. Then, twisting and turning, he dragged the boat under.

Misty's crew stood transfixed, hardly daring to believe what they had witnessed. Some of the men floated face down, rising and falling with the swell. Others splashed weakly towards the ship. Capt. Albern watched sombrely.

'Prepare to take them on board, Mr Skeet,' he ordered.

Skeet hesitated. These were men who would have killed without compunction. But he knew the captain would never leave a man to drown. There was no choice; it was their bounden duty to save a life if possible.

'Aye, aye, Skipper,' he responded.

Tam and Thom threw lines to the swimmers. A man grabbed one and started to pull himself towards the ship. Suddenly he disappeared below the water. He surfaced again with such a bloodcurdling shriek that Misty's crew shuddered. It was the last sound he made as the shark attacked a second time. Patches of red tinged the blue of the sea and another man screamed, and then another. The sharks moved in fast – precise and deadly. They struck silently from beneath, and they lunged in a welter of foam from the surface, their mouths of razor sharp teeth gaping wide, their round eyes cold and merciless. Momentarily the sea seethed with the ferocity of the attack, and then suddenly there were no more screams, no flailing arms and no cries for help. A boot with half a leg in it bobbed to the surface. A sickle shaped fin cut through the water, and then that too was gone.

Ancell clung to the rail. He wanted to walk away, but his legs wouldn't work. He stared at the sea, rising and falling languidly, indifferent to the killing. Only the slowly widening circle of blood marked the slaughter.

'They're efficient, I'll give them that,' muttered Chad with a shiver.

Like automatons, the crew silently gathered on the quarterdeck, seeking the company of each other and the reassurance of standing by their captain at the helm. Doc peered up from the companionway. 'I heard shots. What's happening?' he demanded. Everyone stared at him blankly.

'It's all over,' said Skeet eventually.

'What's over? Have I missed something?'

'Just a few sharks,' said Jobey.

'Why didn't anyone tell me, I'd have liked to have seen them,' complained Doc.

'They were on business – didn't stop to chat,' said Pickle.

'Can the children come up? The gunfire scared them.'

'Bring them up, they've nothing to fear now,' said Capt. Albern.

Suddenly a great bellow erupted as Hector rose from the water. He crashed down in a cascade of spray, then charged back and forth across the entrance of the creek, head and tail lifted, his body inflated and his mouth agape. Drops of water danced from his back as he vibrated with growls and roars.

'He's telling everyone he's king around here,' Doc explained.

'Looks like a victory celebration to me,' said Skeet with a grin.

'Three cheers for Hector!' cried Chips.

Jobey struck the ship's bell repeatedly. Pickle rushed to the galley and grabbed a saucepan and ladle, which he banged above his head, and soon everyone else was doing the same. The children tumbled on deck to call goodbye, Capt. Albern dipped Misty's ensign in respect, and they all yelled, banged and waved farewell to the crocodile. With a final bellow of acknowledgement and a slap of his tail, Hector slipped below the surface, and the only sound was the creak of Misty's rigging.

Laughing Jack and Scarletta burst from the trees, breathless and exhausted from battling through the forest to keep Misty in sight, only to watch her drift seaward and beyond their reach. Choking with anger, his veins pulsing, Laughing Jack dashed his musket to the ground.

'I'll get you! You'll not defy me!' he screamed.

He had watched the sinking of the canoes, and listened to the despairing cries of his crew, but hearing the children's calls of farewell most filled him with fury. He turned on Scarletta. 'They must have got them on board when you were meant to be keeping watch,' he snarled.

'I told you I saw no boat,' snapped Scarletta.

'We'll board "The Executioner" and chase them. We'll blow that ship out of the water.'

Scarletta stroked her cheek, feeling the scar pulse with blood. 'I want to watch those animals die as much as you do,' she said, 'but we've just lost half our crew. We're not in a position to chase anybody.'

Laughing Jack picked up his gun with a trembling hand and fired hopelessly in the direction of Misty.

'You'll not escape me! I won't forget!' he bellowed.

Misty heeled to the first catspaws of wind ruffling the water and her crew braced the yards to the breeze that set in from the north.

'Everything secure, Mr Skeet?' asked Capt. Albern. The second mate thought for a moment and slapped his head with annoyance.

'Sorry, Skipper!' he replied, and ran for'ard, calling for help to make fast the anchor.

Pleased to be at sea again, everyone worked with a will. Skeet announced the first watch, but none of the crew was inclined to rest below and one and all wandered aft to join the children leaning on the stern rail. Together they watched the shoreline recede.

'Goodbye Jandamarra and Hector, and good luck to both of you,' said Skeet, and everyone murmured their agreement.

'And goodbye and to hell with Laughing Jack and Scarletta,' added Chad.

'I hope so, I really do hope so,' said Ancell.

Sassy and Chantal giggled and pointed to Doc perched at the bow, his one good wing outstretched like a lop-sided figurehead, the ends of Waff's bandage streaming in the wind.

'Come back aft! What are you doing up there!' called Chad.

'Can you see land yet?' yelled Pickle.

Doc relaxed his pose and eyed them sternly.

'If you must know, I'm following Hector's recommendation to get some air to my wound, or have you forgotten I've recently been shot?'

'In which case it would be a pleasure to lash you there permanently,' offered Waff, still smarting at Doc's miraculous recovery.

The exchange ended when Misty mischievously dipped her bow and Doc fell over.

'Mind your head!' shouted Waff joyfully.

'Look!' said Max, grabbing Sassy and Chantal with excitement, 'the land – it's nearly out of sight. We really are free!'

Noname stood alone at the foot of the foremast. He was not looking back but up at the billowing canvas, his eyes dancing with delight.

Ancell limped to join him. 'Misty will see us safely home,' he said.

'I'd like this ship to be my home forever,' said Noname, and for the first time Ancell saw him truly smile.

Soaring high above the creek, the sea eagle watched Misty and her extended family heel towards the rim of the horizon, a white dot on an ocean of blue, a world of her own tracking her joyful course homeward. The eagle also spied Hector snoozing on a mud bank and swooped down to annoy him.

THE TOPSAIL SCHOONER 'MISTY DAWN' SAIL PLAN

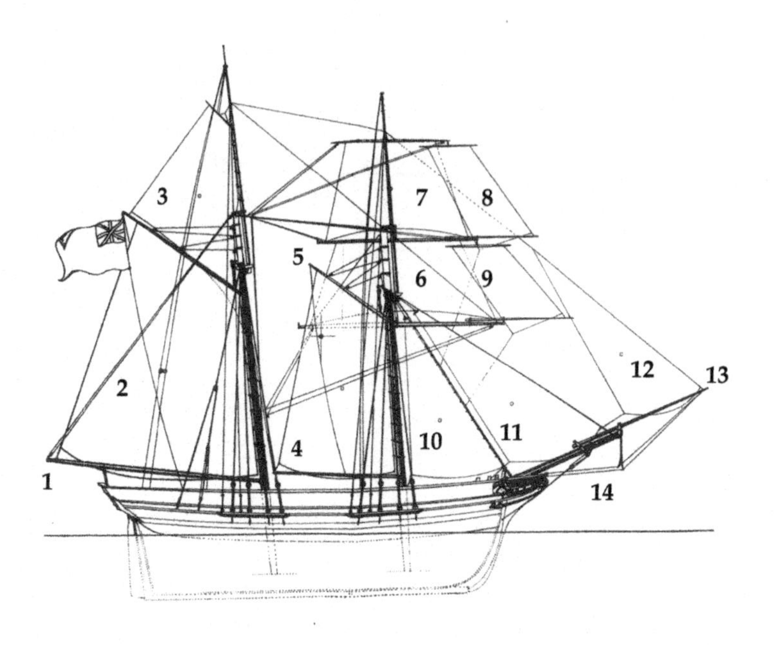

1	Boom	8	Stunsail
2	Mainsail	9	Stunsail
3	Gaff Topsail	10	Foresail
4	Fore Spencer	11	Staysail
5	Gaff	12	Jib
6	Topsail	13	Bowsprit
7	Topgallant	14	Bobstay